ABERDEENSHIRE
LIBRARIES

WITHDRAWN
FROM LIBRARY

Aberdeenshire Library and Information Service
www.aberdeenshire.gov.uk.libraries
Renewals Hotline 01224 661511

ABERDEENSHIRE
LIBRARIES

WITHDRAWN
FROM LIBRARY

3 0 OCT 2015

- 8 AUG 2019
2 6 NOV 2019

ABERDEENSHIRE
LIBRARIES

WITHDRAWN
FROM LIBRARY

-6 JAN 2020
2 5 JUN 2022

3 0 NOV 2022

0 7 FEB 2023

DUNKLE, Clare B.

The walls have eyes

Also by Clare B. Dunkle

The Sky Inside

THE WALLS HAVE EYES

CLARE B. DUNKLE

This book is copyright under the Berne Convention.

The right of Clare B. Dunkle to be identified as the author of this work has been asserted by her in accordance with sections 77 and 78 of the Copyright, Designs and Patents Act 1988.

This book is a work of fiction. Names, characters, places and incidents are either the product of the author's imagination or used fictitiously. Any resemblance to actual people, living or dead, is entirely coincidental.

SIMON AND SCHUSTER

First published in Great Britain in 2009 by
Simon & Schuster UK Ltd
1st Floor, 222 Gray's Inn Road, London WC1X 8HB
A CBS COMPANY

Originally published in 2009 by
Atheneum Books for Young Readers,
An imprint of Simon & Schuster
Children's Publishing Division, New York

Text copyright © 2009 by Clare B. Dunkle

ABERDEENSHIRE LIBRARY AND INFORMATION SERVICES	
2667194	
HJ	2547047
JF	£6.99
JU	JF

Th[...]n.

The r[...]athor
of this wo[...]sections
77 and[...]1988.

This [...]aces
and inci[...]gination
or are us[...]le living
or dead, events or locales is entirely coincidental.

A CIP catalogue record for this book
is available from the British Library.

ISBN: 978-1-84738-479-9

1 3 5 7 9 10 8 6 4 2

Printed by CPI Cox & Wyman, Reading, Berkshire RG1 8EX

www.simonandschuster.co.uk

FOR
EUGENE,

WHO
COULDN'T
WAIT TO
READ MY
BOOKS

THE WALLS HAVE EYES

PROLOGUE

"She's melted down? Completely?"

"We couldn't save a single chip."

One old man and two young men sat on folding chairs in a lemon yellow cube of a room six feet long and six feet high. So close was the space that the knees of their gray pinstripe suits almost touched. With its cheerful color, the room bore a resemblance to a hollowed-out baby's block, but the grim expressions on the faces of the men indicated that playtime was far from their minds. In fact, the baby's block was a clean room, a small space free of bugs or any other spying device. Director Montgomery was taking no chances.

"I conducted the interview myself," Montgomery continued. "The collector bot had failed to bring in her target, a suburban boy named Martin Glass. Five minutes after the collector arrived in our facility, a top priority order came through from Central to melt her at once. I'd barely started the interview when she went into shutdown."

"Pardon me, Director," said one of the young men, "but I don't see why that's such a surprise. The collector had failed. She was malfunctioning. No wonder she was scrapped."

"Thank you for that brilliant insight, Zebulon," Montgomery said. "But I do have some small amount of intelligence, and I thought of that myself. I responded that we understood the demolition order, but we needed time to hold the exit interview. That time was emphatically denied. Yes, the collector had something to tell, and we weren't supposed to hear it. That's what was going on."

He sighed. His colleagues sighed too. Then all three scratched the tips of their noses.

Montgomery was in his sixties, and Zebulon and his partner were in their twenties. Nevertheless, they bore an uncanny resemblance to one another, and not just because of their gray suits. They were clones, duplicates of an operative who had become Agency Director some seventy years ago. That chief had realized his management troubles would be over if his entire workforce thought the same way he did. He had filled the Agency with copies of himself, and his copies had done in-house cloning ever since.

Montgomery leaned toward the two young men with whom he shared a complete set of DNA and an unaccountable fondness for spicy burritos. "Now, you listen to me, Abel, and you do as you're told for a change, Zebulon. Don't repeat this next bit of information once you leave the clean room. Shortly after the meltdown, the Secretary of State contacted my office and asked about 'that Martin Glass boy.' It seems he wanted to interview the collector himself."

"Then you mean—"

"That's right. He didn't know the collector was gone. When I told him she'd been scrapped, he cussed me for a fool. He thought I'd ordered the meltdown. Boys, this looks like a secret plot hatched in the highest levels of government. And for once, the Secretary of State didn't do the hatching."

The two young agents exchanged identical worried looks. "And that means you want us to—"

"That's right! Find out what's going on. I want to know whatever it is that the Secretary of State doesn't know. A little secret plotting is good for this fine nation, but the Agency needs to be in on the joke. If the Secretary has the bad luck to get himself assassinated, we need to be ready to congratulate the winners."

Abel glanced at Zebulon and cleared his throat. "Um . . . doesn't the Secretary demand our absolute loyalty, sir?"

"They all demand our absolute loyalty," Montgomery answered, "right up to the minute they're dead. Now, I don't have much for you to go on. Aside from the boy's name, we only have one decent clue. The packet chief who was present at the failed collection of Martin Glass reported that there was the boy, and then there was a copy of the boy. I thought the copy might have been a hologram, or even the packet chief's imagination, so that was the first question I put to the collector. She confirmed that the copy was there. But get this: 'My canine colleague'—*that's* what she called it."

"'Colleague'?" Zebulon mused. "I thought collectors worked alone."

"'Canine'?" Abel said. "Sir, you can't mean—you don't mean a *dog*?"

"Agent Abel, I don't mean anything," Montgomery said severely. "I just repeat what I hear. It's up to you two to put the meaning into it. Now get out there and find out what's going on!"

Meanwhile, several hundred miles from the clean room, in a secret mountain hideaway that had become the Wonder Baby school, Martin Glass sat on the cafeteria floor and hugged his bot dog. The ecstatic German shepherd bestowed such a frenzy of swipes to Martin's face that the hair that normally fell into his eyes defied gravity for the rest of the day.

Martin's new friend Theo shook her head in disbelief at the hysterical reunion. "How did you manage to get your hands on that superbot, anyway?" she asked.

"Birthday present," Martin said. "Chip, get your nose out of my eye. Settle down. I'm fine!"

Chip flopped onto the floor to beg for a tummy rub and nearly knocked Martin over. *I love you more than anything*, his dark eyes told Martin. *You are my whole world.*

"So you got him by accident," Theo said. "Modified bots cost a fortune. That's somebody's very expensive mistake."

"Don't listen to her, Chip," Martin said. "You're not a mistake. You're my dog—the best dog in the world."

CHAPTER ONE

A month ago Martin Glass had been a regular kid under the steel dome of Suburb HM1, a boy who loved his computer games and hated school. But that had been before his thirteenth birthday, when his parents had given him Chip. The German shepherd could do illegal things, and he had taken Martin to places where no one was allowed to go. There, Martin had learned what happened to the people who didn't do what the government wanted. They were put on the televised game shows, where they played until they lost— and died.

But that wasn't the worst of it. Martin's six-year-old sister, Cassie, was in danger. Cassie was a Wonder Baby, a new and improved model of child. Because of Martin's discoveries about the harshness that lurked below the comfortable surface of his society, he had been very suspicious when a fast-talking stranger had taken Cassie and the other Wonder Babies out of the suburb. Even though the stranger had promised to take care of the little children, something hadn't felt right. When Martin had learned a few days later that the government wanted to ban the Wonder Babies as unsafe consumer products, he had been furious and very worried. He had decided to find out if his sister was all right.

Martin's dog Chip had helped him escape from the suburb, and Martin had found Cassie, safe in a secret school run by the young scientist, Dr. Rudolph Church. Rudy was the prototype for the Wonder Babies, and he thought of them as his little brothers and sisters. When the government had decided to destroy them, Rudy had left his lab to rescue them.

Martin didn't fit in with the supersmart Wonder Babies, and he didn't get along with most of the other geniuses from Rudy's lab. But he had met someone he did get along with: Theo, the prototype for his own product line. When she had invited Martin along on an adventure to find a safer location for the Wonder Baby school, Martin had agreed to go.

Martin and Theo spent the afternoon in the cafeteria, packing their backpacks and preparing for their trip to find a new school for the Wonder Babies. Theo's approach to packing was considerably more thorough than Martin's had been. "We both need medical supplies," she said, dividing up the piles, "in case a pack gets lost."

"I guess that'll be yours," Martin said. "I'm not gonna lose my pack."

"What if it falls in a river? What if wild animals grab it? You remember that it's dangerous outside, right?"

Martin's imagination glossed over the dangers of the untamed wilderness and lingered on the exciting elements instead: beautiful birds, fascinating insects, and the constantly changing scenery. "Sure, I know. So, where do you think we're gonna find a new school, anyway? This one looks pretty good to me."

Theo picked up a small round mirror and squinted into it. Then she swiveled it so Martin caught a glimpse of her stubby nose and bright hazel eyes. "It's too good," she said.

"It's perfect, in fact. That means any agent with access to top secret maps will eventually notice this facility and come here to check it out. We need something we can build or develop ourselves."

"Build where?" Martin asked.

Theo was counting out energy bars. "I have ideas, but we shouldn't discuss them," she said. "There could be bugs even in here."

Martin glanced at the bland white walls, at the ceiling with its broad square panels and big institutional lights. He didn't catch the glitter of light bouncing off tiny glass spying devices, but his spirits sank at the thought. He pictured one of those small gelatinous blobs gliding along the baseboards, distributing its hidden load of bugs. Would he ever get to a place where the walls didn't listen and watch?

"Maybe whoever sets the bugs doesn't care about looking for you," he said. "They were gonna recall the Wonder Babies and take them away from their parents. You guys did that, so now they don't have to. It's like you did them a favor."

Theo grinned. "I'd like to tell the suits at Central that. 'We were just helping you out!' But listen, it was somebody's job to collect those little kids. If I know this government, somebody's still trying to do it."

"What do they want with them?" Martin asked. "What would they do with a bunch of preschool geniuses?"

"Nothing good," Theo said. "Let's hope we don't have to find out."

Dinnertime came, and the cafeteria filled with savory smells. Then it filled with hundreds of adorable little children in blue T-shirts and jeans. Cassie pelted over to him and threw her skinny arms around his waist. "You're still here! My teacher told me I could have dinner with you."

Martin hugged her back. "I'm leaving tomorrow," he said.

"I know. You and Theo are going to search for our new school. But you'll be back when you find it. This is my big brother," she bragged to the nearby children. "He came all the way out here to visit me."

Martin sat down to share a meal of vegetable soup and cheese crackers with her.

"There sure are a bunch of you Wonder kids," he said. "You wouldn't all fit in our school back home."

"This isn't even half of us," Cassie told him as she licked the salt off her crackers. "We eat in shifts, and the toddlers have their own cafeteria. They take naps in it too."

"How do they get enough food for this crowd?"

"They steal it off the packet lines."

"Man! I bet that makes the packet chiefs mad!"

Cassie selected the middle cracker from the stack on her napkin and balanced a piece of sodden zucchini on top of it. "Rudy says we're not supposed to worry about it. He says children should just play and learn. I'm learning a language people used to speak before our language developed. Do you want to hear some of it?"

"No!" Martin said. "That's just nuts. Who cares how a bunch of dead guys talked?"

Cassie shrugged. "I do. Will you be here for breakfast?"

"No. Theo wants to get an early start."

"That's good. You'll find our new school faster," Cassie said.

"Then we won't have to keep tear gas masks in the classrooms anymore and waste time on evacuation drills."

Martin was too shocked to comment.

One by one, the teachers called their classes to turn in their trays and line up. The aisles between the tables were packed solid with the waist-high mob, and Chip crawled under the bench to escape being stepped on. A teenager with a wispy goatee clapped, and Cassie stood up. "That's Pascal, my teacher," she explained. "He was supposed to get his own product line last year, but the government wouldn't let them start incubating the babies. Pascal says they knew then that they were in trouble."

Martin didn't think Pascal looked like much of an improvement over regular people. He was a little too handsome, like a singer for a boy band. Not like William. Now, she was an improvement! But Martin remembered William laughing at him and scowled.

"Don't be sad," Cassie said. "I'm sorry I have to leave, but Pascal says you'll be back in five days. That's not very long."

Martin started to tell her that he wasn't scowling about her, but then he stopped himself. He had already made her cry once today, and besides, he didn't want her to know the real reason. So he let her give him another hug and tugged the golden corkscrew curls on her head.

"You're right," he said. "I'll see you soon."

"Bye, Chip," Cassie said, and the German shepherd poked his head out from under the table to have his ears scratched. "Take care of my big brother for me." Then she joined the students lining up next to Pascal and marched out of the cafeteria.

The next shift of Wonder Babies swarmed in. Martin spotted Jimmy talking to some boys from his class. If it hadn't been for the piebald rat on Jimmy's shoulder, Martin wouldn't have recognized the tanned, happy boy as the harassed child he had rescued from a beating. They're so pretty, Martin thought, but it went beyond that, in a way he couldn't put into words. Maybe they really were new and improved human beings.

Martin wandered over to Theo and their backpacks, thinking about Dad. Dad had convinced the parents of his suburb to send their Wonder Babies to the school, but only because he thought he was helping the government get rid of them. Dad had sold out his own daughter to keep things cozy for himself, and Martin was the only one who knew.

"Whose murder are you planning?" Theo asked as Martin walked up.

"My dad's," he muttered.

"Been there. I had sixteen dads, you know. The plans got very elaborate. Okay, we're finished here. I need to go review some codes for Rudy. We're this close to hacking Central's com protocol so we can intercept messages about us."

"Do they really need tear gas masks?" Martin wanted to know. "The little kids, I mean?"

Theo paused to study his face before she answered.

"Oh, you know how it is," she said lightly. "Better safe than sorry. Listen, tell Sim when he comes by to get you a place to sleep. But don't let him put you in the dorm, or you'll be up all night listening to chess problems. Lordy! I do hate chess!"

She left, and Martin loitered in the cafeteria. She didn't answer my question, he thought. Even Theo doesn't tell me things.

The second shift of Wonder Babies turned in their trays and left. With nothing else to do, Martin checked his knapsack again. The fact that this was a school deterred him from wandering the halls. Wandering school hallways got you yelled at. The bare room and white laminate tables depressed him. Did schools ever look nice?

"I thought I'd find you here."

William stood in the doorway. She was as gorgeous as ever, and now Martin knew she was terrifically smart as well. "Sim says you're leaving in the morning," she said. "Off with Theo to find a new site for the school."

Hey, maybe she came to wish me luck, Martin thought. I should say something. After all, she's a teenager like me. But he didn't, because she wasn't. She might be his age, but she was a genius like the rest of the prototypes. He remembered how she had performed an experiment on him to see what he'd do if she swiped his shoes. She seemed to like making fun of him.

"I was hoping you'd do me a favor if you have the time," William said. "Can you help me with a tool that's out of reach?"

"Oh, sure," Martin said. "Come on, Chip."

William led the way through the empty, impersonal corridors to her office. Following William was rapidly becoming the best part of Martin's day. Her shiny brown hair looks just like when syrup meets butter, Martin thought, and there isn't a more beautiful sight than that.

The office was an even greater disaster now than it had been earlier. Martin stepped gingerly around a cardboard box full of old circuit boards. Chip sniffed at them and gave an unhappy whine.

"It's okay, boy," Martin told him. "They aren't anybody you know."

William waded through the piles and stacks to a shelving unit in the far corner. "Up there," she said as she stood on her tiptoes in her high-tops and pointed to an object on the highest shelf.

The object she wanted was about a foot square, wrapped in a hard case of dusty green. From its front protruded many short metal bits that gave it a snaggletoothed bulldog's grin.

"What is it?"

"An antique," she said. "A typewriter."

"Is it heavy?"

"That depends on your idea of heavy."

Martin stretched as far as he could, but he could barely brush the typewriter's bottom edge with his fingertips. He decided against dislodging it and walking it off the shelf inch by inch; his idea of heavy was an object capable of bashing his head in, and this one looked as if it could. He glanced around. The office chair rolled, so that was no good. He picked his way back through the mess and began moving boxes off the chair by the door.

"What are you doing?"

Martin gestured at the chair. "What does it look like I'm doing?"

"You'll get those out of order," William said. "I have a system." And she frowned when Martin laughed. "Anyway, you don't need that chair. Think! You have another way."

Now it was Martin's turn to frown. "I don't need to think, and I don't need another way. The chair's my way, so if you don't want me to move it, it looks like you and that typer thingy are out of luck."

William nodded as if he'd just confirmed her suspicions about something. Then she went to the door.

"Sim," she called, "would you come here for a minute and fetch me down the typewriter?"

The bent old bot hobbled to the doorway. His mild blue eyes brightened when he saw Martin. "Oh, hello, new student. Taking a little instruction, I see."

William's laugh annoyed Martin much more than it should have.

With some difficulty and adjustment of his gray robes to avoid toppling papers, Sim made his way across the room. Then he reached up one skinny arm. It stretched to an absurd length in a sudden movement that made Martin's stomach flop over. Foot-long fingers fanned wide and plucked the cumbersome object from the shelf.

"Here you are," Sim said, turning toward them with the typewriter in his arms. "Where would you like me to put it?"

"Just put it back," William said. "I don't need it today."

The old man lifted it back into place with the same impossibly elastic ease. Then he turned to go. "Pay no mind. I'm just a bot," he said sadly to Martin as he passed. "It doesn't matter if *I* understand what's going on."

"So this was another one of your experiments," Martin fumed when Sim was gone. "Look, if you wanna laugh at me, go ahead and laugh. You don't need an excuse."

THE WALLS HAVE EYES

"I'm not laughing at you," William said. "I thought we might both learn something. When you couldn't reach the typewriter, all you needed to do was ask your bot to take it down. Why didn't you think of that?"

Martin swiveled in place. Chip stood behind him, up to his pasterns in paper stacks. When his dark eyes met Martin's, his ears folded back in a friendly greeting, and his tail set up a confetti whirl.

"Stop it! Stop him!" William cried. "He's messing up my system!"

"Oh, forget your system," Martin said, ruffling Chip's ears. "A dog's gotta wag."

"He doesn't wag because he's a dog," William said. "He wags because you want him to. He's a modified bot—a super-machine. His programming must be extensive. You're keeping him from reaching his full potential by encouraging him to be a dog."

Martin turned on her. "What is it with you people? Why do you keep harping on about him not being a dog? Let's go, Chip. You're messing up her system."

William followed him out into the hall. "Maybe he's an important machine," she said earnestly. "A much more powerful bot."

"He's powerful like he is," Martin said as he turned the corner. The sterile hallway stretched out before him, its floor tiles yellow-green and bilious. The sense of being back at the school sapped his spirits. Where was that cafeteria, anyway?

William persisted. "But he could be so much more!"

Another corner, and floor tiles that were blue with brown flecks. He was on the right track now. Down the hall, a door stood open, with white wheeled trestle tables beyond it. Martin spotted his knapsack with a feeling of relief. I can't wait to get out of this place, he thought.

"Chip's my dog," he said. "Maybe that's not good enough for you, but it's good enough for me. If you think I'm gonna let you change him into some kind of monster battle bot, you're out of your mind."

"I don't know if he's supposed to be a battle machine," William said. "We need to find out what he is."

Chip gave a yelp and dashed past Martin. Martin turned to see what had scared the dog. William was holding a reset chip in her hand.

"No way!" Martin said, snatching the chip from her. "Nobody resets him. He hates it."

William sighed. "You've anthropomorphized him."

"Whatever." Martin made his way over to the supplies and tossed the chip into his knapsack. "You had all afternoon to check him out while he was charging, so don't think I'm gonna feel bad for you now."

"But I didn't," William protested. "I was in class. Rudy told Sim not to release your bot to you, but when Sim heard Rudy praise you for being a credit to your designer, Sim decided he didn't need to obey the release order anymore. Sim has design flaws. He doesn't always do what he's supposed to."

Martin thought of the schizophrenic welcome the old bot had given him at the tunnel entrance. "Yeah, I kinda noticed," he said.

"Rudy built him when he was ten," William went on. "I would have done a better job. So I need to see your bot now." She hesitated. "Please? It's very important."

Martin snorted. "Not to me." He regretted this statement almost at once.

"Well, isn't that wonderful!" William snapped. "We ask you for help, and do you want to help us? No, you'd rather coddle a machine!"

"I am too helping," Martin said. "I'm going out there to find a new place for your school."

William rolled her eyes. "Oh, right."

Disappointment bubbled up in Martin's throat, hot and thick. I knew it, he thought. I knew these geniuses didn't need me around.

"I get it," he said bitterly. "Theo doesn't need me along on this trip. No wonder she won't tell me anything. She's just gonna look after the defective kid and give me something to do, and I bet you all think I'll just slow her down. Well, tell her thanks, but I don't need a babysitter. I'll be fine on my own." He grabbed his knapsack and headed for the door.

"What's *wrong* with you?" William demanded, tagging after him down the hallway. "We're all in danger here! Why do you have to make everything into a fight?"

Martin didn't have a good comeback for that, so he ignored it. He pushed through the double doors that opened onto the valley and walked out into the twilight. William stopped at the doors. As far as Martin was concerned, she might as well have stopped a million miles behind him.

Loneliness swept through him. He didn't know where to go

or what to do. But Chip trotted beside him, ears pricked and tail wagging.

Great, we're going somewhere, his dark eyes said. *You know best. What's the plan?*

Martin thought about the people he loved. Cassie was happy with her school friends, and she had Rudy and Theo to look after her. His friends David and Matt probably whispered about how he had disappeared, but they didn't need him. They had each other for company. He pictured Dad at his console with his freight bots, and Mom at the kitchen table. Mom, left all by herself. Of course! He had his plan.

"We'll go rescue Mom," Martin told Chip. "She hates it in that suburb, and she'd love it outside. Anyway, she shouldn't be stuck with Dad anymore. She'd hate him if she knew what he did."

"We're in danger here every minute," William yelled after him as he started off. "Every minute! You know that!"

Martin turned and gave her a sarcastic wave good-bye. "Yeah, well, you've made it pretty obvious that I'm too dumb to know much of anything. But you're the smartest person on the planet. You'll be just fine."

CHAPTER TWO

Martin made good time on the trip home. "I'm getting better at hiking," he told Chip. Besides, he knew exactly where he was going, and that certainty kept him walking late into the evening. Every day that passed was another day Mom spent trapped under the steel dome of Suburb HM1. Martin couldn't wait to get her out of there.

He made only one detour. He had left his favorite sweatshirt in his school backpack at the camp he had shared with Hertz, the blue-eyed outdoorsman bot who had tried to adopt Martin's quest as his own. When Martin saw the high, bare knob of Hertz's hill rising in the distance, he paused to consult with his dog.

"It's chilly in the mornings. I could really use that sweatshirt. It's not that far, and we could take a shortcut through the fields back to the packet line."

Chip crouched down and tucked his tail between his legs.

"Don't be silly!" Martin scolded. "Hertz can't get you anymore. He's nothing but a big wad of silver Jell-O. The reset chip is keeping him that way, and it's not like he can do anything about it."

Martin headed to the high hill that marked the old camp, with his unhappy dog slinking along behind him. But when they got to the camp, Martin's backpack wasn't there. Neither was Hertz. They could plainly see the broken weeds where the big bot had flailed in agony, but his oblong of silver gel was gone.

Martin ran from the spot. When he couldn't run anymore, he trotted. Then he ran again, as far and as fast as he could, sure that the killer bot was on his trail. Not until the next morning dawned, clear and tranquil, did he begin to feel safe again.

"We're never going back there, Chip," he said. "Never! Hertz can keep that whole place for himself." And the thought of the strong, rugged bot striding alone through the empty hills sent a shiver down Martin's spine.

By noon on the third day, Martin spotted the steel dome of HM1 by noon on the third day, a bright gleam of light on the top of a far off hill. As the afternoon wore on, it grew larger, and its dazzling glare intensified, until Martin couldn't look straight at it anymore. When the sun sank, its light struck up a ruddy glow from the steel structure, as if Martin's former home were on fire. And in the fading colors after sunset, Martin reached the cinder-block fence that surrounded the suburb's dome.

"It's so weird, Chip," he said. "It's all in there. Families, playgrounds, the store, the bowling alley, all stuck inside this big bubble. It's like a package of army men or something, like a kit with a bunch of parts."

The German shepherd didn't appear to be paying attention to Martin. He kept looking back and swiveling his tall ears to take in the sounds of the coming night.

"Okay," Martin said. "Dad's gone home. The main thing is to check the loading bay for one of those transmitter things. If there isn't one, we know an inspection isn't going on, and that means nobody's looking at us through all those little glass eyes. We'll keep quiet in case they're listening, though, and we'll head to the factory. Bug hid out there, and nobody heard him for two whole years, so we'll be fine for tonight."

Chip licked Martin's hand, glanced over his shoulder, and gave a breathy little whine.

"Would you quit worrying?" Martin said. "We'll be back outside with Mom by this time tomorrow. Now, let's get in fast before that security bot finds us here. I don't want him setting off some alarm."

Chip transformed into a rolling dog and carried Martin in on the packet rails. Obeying Martin's instruction, he picked up quite a bit of speed. It was all Martin could do to hang on.

They whizzed through the long tunnel and through the dark washing room. The sprinklers exploded in a downpour behind them, but the big steel doors were already swinging open, and only a shower of drops caught them as they sped into the loading bay.

The big banks of fluorescent tubes were off for the night. Four small emergency lamps shed a golden glow at the edges of the gloomy space. The shadows of the freight bots were enormous as the bots rolled forward to greet them.

"No transmitter," Martin whispered, pointing up into the gloom. "Chip, get these guys to back off, and let's get out of here."

They made their way to the hall with the raveled red rug and the door marked AUTHORIZED ENTRANCE ONLY. Then the German shepherd covered the keypad with his paw and broke its code. Martin pushed the door open, and they stepped into the nighttime world beneath the suburb, the unlit access space that held the tanks and conduits linked to the houses on the level above.

Chip lit his eyes, and their twin beams shone out into the massive basement, flickering across its concrete columns and cement floor. Booming, hissing industrial noises surrounded them as they walked. A tiny flame at the ceiling attracted their attention. A tool bot clung there, welding a metal pipe.

Fifteen minutes later, they reached the factory and hurried through its well-lit passages to the managers' break room. The big television still blared, and Bug's little colored disks still lay on the brown tabletop. The custodial bots appeared to be dusting around them.

"Poor Bug," Martin said at the sight of the crazy man's solitaire game. "He wasn't hurting anybody with his jokes and wild ideas. Do you think he's still alive?"

Chip made a circuit of the room, sniffing. Then he laid his ears back and leaned into Martin, who stroked his ruff.

"Yeah, I know. You can't tell. I bet Bug was right. I bet they put him on the game shows. You know, it's a pretty creepy government that kills you just for having a big mouth."

Chew your way to health! babbled the television. *It's a vitamin and a gum.*

Martin found the remote and changed the channel.

The break room cooker offered him the choice of hot pastrami on rye with a pickle on the side, pepperoni pizza and carrot sticks, or a jumbo Caesar salad. The fridge held nothing but low-calorie soda.

"I can't believe Bug was stuck eating this stuff for two years," Martin said. "And no candy, either. I don't know how he stood it."

Martin ordered up several pizza slices and flipped channels on the television. There was nothing on. He wandered around the factory, looking for a good place to sleep, but jaunty music played over the speakers, and a bot in the corridor startled him by turning on its vacuum. Martin returned to the break room.

At ten o'clock, the television picture winked out with an indefinable crackle that Martin had always associated with dying. He spread out his bedroll in the corner and tried to turn off the break room light. It didn't have a switch. None of the factory lights did. A custodial bot rolled in, wadded up his empty pizza trays, and began wiping down the counters.

"Mom and Dad are in bed now," Martin said, grabbing his knapsack and stuffing the bedroll into it. "And we're not getting any sleep down here till the cleaning brigade is done. I need to charge my game cartridges if I'm gonna take them with me this time. Now's a perfect time to go grab them."

They left through the factory lobby with its polished granite tiles, climbed the wide marble steps to the suburb level, and crept out into the park. Street lamps shone down on the asphalt path, but the rest of the park was in shadow. The empty space stretched away from them, devoid of sound or movement. Not a cricket chirped in the darkness.

Martin looked up. The night felt close, and the air seemed stale. The steel dome above him blocked out the stars. Nighttime in the suburb. He hated it here.

"Mom's gonna love it outside," he whispered to Chip. "I wish I could talk David and Matt into coming too, but I don't wanna make their parents mad. Besides, Matt would try to bring his whole collection of celebrity batting helmets with him. We'd need a rolling dumpster just to haul them around."

Orange streetlights illuminated the curving row of houses before him. Not forty feet from Martin stood his own house and his own front door. It looked so ordinary, it took his breath away.

Chip opened that door, and they sneaked into the front hall. A tiny night-light was on, and everything was quiet. Foraging by the light of the open fridge, Martin grabbed a strawberry-kiwi soda and a bag of barbecue puffs. Then he tiptoed down the hall to his room.

Mom had been in here, putting things away. Martin's bed was made, and he could see the surface of his desk. But his faithful beanbag chair was still in a heap by the rug, and his box of game cartridges lay within easy reach. Martin shut the door and flipped on his plasma lamp.

The purple-and-green paisley shapes of the plasma lamp swirled around the darkened room, fat and slow on the walls, thin and hurried in the corners. They looked like clouds, he realized. They weren't quite as good as clouds, but they were something that changed, anyway.

Martin rummaged through the box of cartridges as quietly as he could. "Okay, which to take? Speed Addiction, that's a good one, with all the scooter crashes." He set it in the charger. "And which one's this? The label's gone." He flipped the power switch.

An eerie sight flickered into view on the cartridge screen. It was a ruined house bathed in twilight shades of velvet blue and charcoal gray. Martin felt the hair prickle on his arms.

"House-to-House Six," he murmured. "That looks like the places we saw in the old suburb outside." More tumbledown houses floated across the screen, stark black against a lurid sky. Red eyes blinked from the gap of a doorway. Martin hit the fire button.

"See, this isn't the future, when we're all mutants," he whispered in excitement. "This is how it is right now! I bet these things are the stuff that's haunting those abandoned suburbs, all those people the President killed when he built the domes. The guys who made this game must have been out there and seen them."

His player stumbled, and the screen lit up with vomit green streaks. Three zombies in ragged jeans were attacking him with knives. He turned and fired just in time, then ran past their wriggling limbs.

"I didn't recognize it because I was there in the daytime, and these pictures don't show the bushes and stuff. Besides, I bet these things hide when it's light outside. We were lucky we got out before night."

A green skeleton glided into view. Martin fired, but it kept coming. "Grenade!" he said, hitting buttons, and the skeleton burst into a shower of fragments. "I bet the government ordered up these games to train commandos. I better study up on these things!"

The door clicked as it opened. Chip scrambled to his feet and barked. Mom and Dad stood in the doorway, mouths open and eyes wide.

CHAPTER THREE

The plasma lamp's purple and green clouds drifted across his parents' stunned faces. Martin dropped the cartridge with a clatter. He thought Mom and Dad looked just like zombies.

Then Mom wrapped her arms around him in a hug so tight it hurt.

Dad's face was a collage of different emotions. "How— What—"

"Don't ask, Walt," Mom warned. "The walls have ears." Then she hugged Martin again.

Martin looked away from Dad's face.

"I'm hungry, Mom," he said. "Got any good cereal in the house?"

A few minutes later, he was sitting at his old spot at the kitchen table. In the middle of the table was a doily, and on it Mom's lazy Susan, which she'd made in plate-painting class: THE KITCHEN TABLE IS THE HEART OF THE HOME.

Mom took his chin in her hands and tilted his face toward the light. "Martin, your face," she said softly. "What happened to you out there?"

"Sun," Martin said, reaching for the milk and pouring it onto the cereal. "It burns you, but you peel and get a whole new set of skin. Browner, too. See?" He exhibited his arms.

"And you're so dirty! How did you manage to get so dirty?"

"There's a whole lot of dirt out there, Mom."

Martin scooped up the jewel-colored nuggets in eight bites

and dumped in another round. His parents sat down to watch him eat. He hadn't seen them look at him like that since the day he'd beaten up Principal Thomasson's boy.

"Son," Dad said, "you've done a terrible thing. You've endangered your whole family."

"My whole family's not here," Martin said. "I had to make sure Cassie was all right. And she is, Mom. She's doing great."

His parents' faces blanched with shock again. Dad went back to talking in monosyllables. "How—Where—Did—" Martin was getting a little tired of it.

"I went to Cassie's school, Mom," he said. "I took her her bunny. I told her you hoped she was doing math, and she was, too. She told me this crazy stuff about quadratic thingies and tesla somethings; I didn't get much out of it. But their school isn't all that safe. In fact, I better not talk about it. You know, because of the walls."

Mom dropped her face into her hands and started to cry. Dad looked confused and gloomy, and maybe a little guilty. Yeah, that's right, Martin thought with satisfaction. You think about what you did. You think about how you sent your daughter away to die.

"Martin," Dad said sternly, "your mother's been through a lot. She doesn't need you to break her heart with playground stories. We need you to tell us the truth."

"Okay, now, the truth," Martin said. "You know, it's funny you bring up the truth, because I know a guy who turned the truth into a trick. He was a scientist who lived in the laboratory where the Wonder Babies were made and that's why he knew so much about them. He made *some* people think he was working for the recall, and then he took all the Wonder Babies away to his school before the recall people could get them."

Dad looked away and fell silent.

Martin left Dad sitting at the table and followed his mom down the hall. She pulled pajamas out of the drawer and laid them on his bed for him as if he were four years old, straightening the sleeves and smoothing out the wrinkles with trembling hands. Martin scooped up the pajamas before she could turn them into a still life.

"You'd better take a shower," she said. "All that dirt!" And she stared at him with wonder in her eyes. Martin closed the bathroom door on her before she could arrange his towels for him and make him feel even stranger than he already did.

Out in the hall again after the shower, he heard his parents in Cassie's room. He waved for Chip to wait for him and tiptoed to Cassie's door. Why? He didn't know. Years of habit. Long years of sitting in the hall night after night and listening to his parents' conversation.

Mom was tidying Cassie's room even though it was already tidy, making little still lifes out of her dolls and games. "Isn't it wonderful?" she said. "We've got our boy back. I feel as if I fell asleep and dreamt it."

Dad was standing over her, watching. He shifted and cleared his throat.

"Tris, I know what you want me to say," he muttered. "But we haven't got him back."

Mom whirled. Martin ducked out of sight just in time. "How can you say that?" she demanded. "Don't you even care?"

"Of course I care." Dad sounded sad. "I wish he were somewhere else, safe. But we can't hide him in his room forever, and he can't go out that door. Central knows he was out of the suburb. They asked me about him just last week."

Mom made no sound.

"The minute they know he's back, they'll collect him," Dad said. "It's as simple as that."

Not before I'm out of here, Martin thought as he tiptoed back to his room.

Seven o'clock the next morning found Martin lying in bed and listening to the national anthem. The swinging rhythm of the grandiose music was impossible to tune out. No birds sang. No wind blew past his face. And there would be no sunrise in here either, he reminded himself ruefully. Just daybreak at the flick of a switch.

Chip yawned and hopped to the floor. Martin sat up and rubbed his eyes. "How did we stand this place, Chip?" he muttered.

Martin wandered out to watch his parents vote on the keypad by the television. At seven thirty, the President appeared behind his podium, black suit impeccable and dark eyes as serious as ever. Martin felt himself straighten up, just as he had done in early childhood when he'd thought that the President was looking at him.

The President thanked his people for their assistance in choosing a new dress uniform for the military bots. Then his handsome face faded into a montage of waving flags. An ad for designer vegetables came on: *Bring cauliflower to the party!* Martin and his parents turned their attention to breakfast.

No one spoke. Dad didn't look as if he'd slept. He propped his cheek against his hand and sipped his coffee out of a mug that said I † MORNINGS.

Just talk to me, Martin thought, watching Dad. I bet you won't do it, you coward.

Mom was in a reverie by the sink, absentmindedly washing her mug. "He seems so sad these days," she said at last.

"Who?" Dad asked.

"The President. He's looked so tired these past few weeks. I think you upset him, voting for that flashy gold braid."

Dad caught sight of what Martin was doing. "Onion squares for breakfast?"

Martin withdrew a handful of squares from the bag and placed them next to a pile of marshmallow cookies. "I had my cereal last night," he pointed out.

Dad stared into his coffee cup while Martin crunched through the onion squares. I dare you to say it, Martin thought.

"Son, we've decided that you'd better stay home from school today. That burned skin doesn't look like it's healed up."

"It's fine," Martin said. "Really." And he settled back to enjoy the worried look that crossed Dad's face.

"Tell you what," Dad said. "I think Mom wanted you to help around the house. Wasn't that right, Tris?"

"Oh, sure, then," Martin said. "Anything for Mom."

Dad went off to shower and get ready for his workday. Martin couldn't wait for him to leave. Then he and Mom could start packing. When Dad came home for lunch, they'd be gone.

That's right! the television assured him. *We've got the shoes, the workout shorts, the wrist weights, the pedometer, the heart computer, the wicking tank top, and the neoprene water bottle! Walk yourself fit! Walk yourself slim! Start walking today for the low, low price of one hundred and ninety-nine dollars.*

"Come on, Chip," Martin said. "Let's check to see if our House-to-House cartridges are charged."

But Martin's game cartridges troubled him with their simulation of the abandoned suburb outside, and the view inside his tiny room began to depress him. He threw himself on his rug to stare at the low ceiling and close walls. I'm stuck in a box, he thought. Hurry up, Dad, leave!

Chip lay down next to Martin and poked his nose into Martin's face. His bushy tail thumped against the carpet.

"I can't wait to get out of here," Martin told him. "I know what's on television—I mean, not exactly, but almost. I know what everybody's doing. It's so boring here. It's not like anything's ever new."

Martin heard Dad's scooter start up outside. But at that same instant, a glimmer above his desk attracted his attention. "Hold on," he breathed. "*That's* new."

An inch-long gelatinous blob, light blue to match his wallpaper, glided along the wall above his desk lamp. It looked like a cross between a grub and a centipede; its fringe of hairlike legs pulsated smoothly. As he leaned in close, it paused briefly to deposit a white dot that gleamed like a tiny eye.

"Oh, no way!" Martin whispered.

He snatched his sneaker from the floor and brought it down hard. The thing dropped onto his desk, squirmed to right itself, and went rippling on its way. Martin smacked it with his sneaker, then raised the shoe to smack it again. But now the desk was empty.

He turned his sneaker over. The thing was hiding in his shoe treads, distributed in thick blue lines among the waffle weaves. As he watched, the lines quivered slightly. Then they popped together with a sound like a snapped piece of bubble gum and bounced into the oval shape once more.

Martin shook it onto the desk. His heart was pounding. "Chip, what do we *do*?"

Chip sniffed at the rubbery form. Then he hid it with a tan paw. After a few seconds, down from his paw sifted a powder of finely ground glass spangled with a few bright metal bits.

Martin scraped the white dot off the wall and dropped it into the trash can. It was sticky. He had to flick it with a thumbnail to get it off his fingers. He found another couple of dots and removed them with difficulty. The remaining dots he couldn't budge.

"Eyeballs," he said while Chip sat in the middle of the floor and studied the fixed dots with interest. "My walls have eyeballs. Again! Well, they're not gonna watch us for long."

He found Mom at the kitchen table peeling an orange. "We've gotta talk," he said. "About the outside."

She glanced over her shoulder. "Martin. The walls."

"I know. And they aren't just listening. They're watching, too. But it doesn't matter. Tell me anything you want. I heard what Dad said. I've gotta leave."

Mom didn't speak. She studied her sections of orange as if they contained a secret code, a little dent forming between her brows. She carefully fitted the sections together, but the minute she moved her hand, they fell apart.

"It's not just because of the walls," Martin said. "Or because I hate Dad, or school, or anything like that. It's amazing out there, Mom. Amazing! You've gotta see it. I came back here to get you."

She glanced up at him with a quizzical smile. "You did?"

"You hate it here," he said. "You'll love it outside. You've gotta come with me!"

"I wish I could, dear," she sighed. But lurking in her eyes was a question: *I couldn't—could I?*

Martin pounced on that hint of uncertainty.

"The sun comes up like a painting, Mom, like a big gorgeous red ball, and it's got clouds around it, all pink and goldy. And the wind blows all the time, hard and soft, and cold sometimes, like it's alive. And there's birds, they sing, and they fly all around you, like—like birds. They come in all colors, sometimes all on one bird. I mean, if you held them and painted them, even if they'd stay still, it'd take you all day to get them right. And trees! Like giant broccoli, kinda—well, more serious than that, I dunno—and they rustle and move like they're happy to see you."

Mom's eyes were alight. She said, "So birds are real?" And Martin knew that his granny had told her secrets once before.

"Birds are everywhere. Thousands. And that's just the start! There's bugs, all colors, running around in the grass, and the grass grows long and waves around in the wind, and there's cactus, with prickles all over it like a hairbrush—I don't know what they're for—and rabbits and ponds and thunderstorms and the moon—oh, the moon!—and you'd never believe the stars."

He fell silent, overwhelmed by his own inadequacy to describe it. Maybe if he had worked harder in school, he'd know the right things to say.

But Mom's eyes were shining. "It would be worth it just to see if it's all true," she said. "Even if I don't live another day."

The door slammed, and Dad trudged in. He opened the fridge and pulled out a beer.

Dad again? It can't be, Martin thought. He just left! Now he'll ruin everything.

"Walt, I've decided," Mom said in a rush. "I'm going outside with Martin, and I'm going to paint birds."

"Really?" Dad said. "Then we'd better hurry. They're coming to get us. We have an hour—maybe two at the most."

CHAPTER FOUR

"Who's coming?" Mom asked.

Martin said, "Wait! But you don't want—I mean, aren't you gonna stay here?"

Dad answered the question that made more sense.

"Agents are on their way," he said. "Not one, but two! And I suppose you've noticed we're in the middle of our own mini-inspection. We've got those damn crawlers all over the house."

"Walt!"

"This is your fault, son," Dad said. "Your fault, Martin Revere Glass. They sent word ahead that they want to discuss my son. Agents want to discuss my son! Do you know what agents do? They make you glad when you get to your game show, that's what agents do!"

Mom made a movement with her hands. "Walt, don't!"

Martin jumped up from the table. Where was his knapsack? That's right, in his bedroom. "Okay, let's go."

Mom pushed the chairs in and fixed the fruit bowl with nervous fingers. "I've got to get my paints," she said. "Martin, what else do we bring?"

"Oh, wow, we'll need more water," Martin said, thinking about it. "We can use empty soda bottles. And energy bars. They taste nasty, but they're the best thing to have."

"Hold on a minute," Dad said. "Can we live out there or not?"

"Well, sure," Martin said. "It's great out there. Birds and trees . . ."

Dad's eyes didn't light up as Mom's had done.

"If we can live out there, then why are we bringing food?"

"Oh! It's just—well, kinda like a shortcut. I mean, there's food and all. There's rabbits—oh, and there's fish. Dad, you'll wanna bring your fishing stuff."

"Fishing?" Dad's face looked a little less grim. "That's good. I'll get the tackle box."

"And a sheet. And a blanket, too. And—Oh, crap! Toilet paper! Mom, you're gonna want lots of that."

Chaos reigned for the next hour. Mom tore through the piles in the garage to find all her paints and a tote to put them in. Dad checked his tackle and crammed supplies into Martin's spare school backpack. Martin raided the pantry for energy bars and stowed a pair of Everlite batteries for Chip.

"Just five more minutes," Mom said when they were done. "Martin, go through the fridge and toss everything down the garbage chute. I won't have my neighbors see this house in a mess."

"I can't. I gotta load the water," Martin said. He was slinging roped pairs of bottles across Chip's back.

Dad's watch began to buzz, and he seemed to shrink a little. "That's it," he said. "We're out of time."

Mom came running from the bedroom when she heard him and put an arm around his waist. "Walt, I'm so sorry," she said. "It's my silly vanity, not wanting to leave our house a mess."

"Hey, whoa, wait a minute," Martin interrupted. "So they're here. It's not like they're *here*."

"Forget it," Dad said. "The agents just pulled into the loading bay. And they probably brought a collector bot, too."

"So what?" Martin said. "I've stood this far from a collector. Look, you can stay here if you want to, but, Mom, grab your stuff and let's get going."

On the doorstep, Martin paused. The scene wasn't as he remembered it. Yes, there was the park across the street, with its green-gravel expanses and its multihued play structures. Overhead hung the massive steel dome with its painted sky and clouds. The big skylights set into its curved surface glowed like giant lamps.

"But was it this dark before?" Martin said. "I feel like my eyes don't work."

None of the colors were right. The steel dome wasn't powder blue. It was dull indigo, and the painted white clouds were gray. The redbrick houses around the street weren't red, either. They were dark burgundy. Everything in the distance blended into gloom.

Mr. LaRue was on his sidewalk, glaring at them. His face seemed to be in shadow.

"Good morning," Mom called to him as she juggled her painting tote and easel. "Just going for a picnic in the park."

Mr. LaRue went into his house and slammed the door.

"What a nasty place," Martin decided, looking at all the ruined colors. "Let's get out of here."

He herded his little group across the street and down a wide asphalt walkway. They stopped at a little building faced with gray stone.

"Chip, unlock the door. Hurry," Martin said. He pulled open the door and waved them inside. Then he led them down into the handsome factory lobby and beyond it into the wide, echoing concrete basement of the suburb. Chip's eyes lit up as he trotted ahead into the darkness.

"That Alldog!" Dad cried, standing still. "Will you look at what he's doing?"

"Yeah, but I like to have my own flashlight just in case. You two need to get moving, really. We have somewhere to get to, you know."

Their shuffling footsteps echoed in the vast space like the sounds of a mutant army. Dad murmured, "I knew there was an access space, but I never imagined it was so tall."

"It's eerie," Mom said. "I keep thinking I'll see ghosts."

Martin remembered Bug. "Actually, Chip and I did see one once."

They came to the door marked AUTHORIZED ENTRANCE ONLY and went through it to the narrow hallway. Martin stopped them on the disreputable red rug.

"Now, you guys stay here," he whispered. "Chip and I are gonna go check out the loading bay. I'm gonna leave this door open. You can go hide in the factory if I get nabbed and collected. It's got its own television, and there's a cooker in there and everything."

He crept to the corner, then turned to look back. Mom and Dad were right behind him.

"What are you doing?" he hissed. "You need to stay put!"

"Sweetie, I can't let you walk into trouble," Mom whispered.

"It's *my* loading bay," Dad said.

They made their way carefully through the corridors. When the last corner before the loading bay was in front of them, Martin stopped them again.

"Now I really have to go by myself," he whispered. "Because if they're walking around in there and we all try to creep up on them, then we might as well all go in playing kazoos." He unroped the pairs of bottles from Chip's back and shrugged off his knapsack. Then he crawled on his hands and knees to the corner and peeked into the bay.

A packet car he'd never seen before stood by the steel gates. Sided with dull maroon corrugated panels, it would have looked just like a regular packet that held boxes for the warehouse if not for the steel door set in its end. Warehouse goods didn't need a door; their packets had removable sides. Only people used a door like that—or bots designed to look like people.

Two young men prowled and paced near the packet car. They wore identical gray suits with blue ties, identical black shoes, and identical expressions of disgust. "Twins," Martin whispered to Chip. He didn't know quite what the word meant, except that it meant two of the same thing. Dolls were sold in pairs as twins, and a famous superhero had split into twins. That made him twice as good at fighting crime.

The twins would have looked ordinary if they hadn't been a matched set. They had unremarkable faces with stubby chins, short noses, and little fish mouths that clapped shut into a frown. Their short hair was blond, and their brows and sparse lashes were pale. Their eyes looked watery and shortsighted.

"Where is he?" snapped the first twin. "Why is he making us wait?"

The second twin hoisted himself up to sit in the doorway of their packet car. The packet didn't have steps or a railing, so his legs dangled a few inches above the ground, pulling up his trouser legs and revealing his white socks. "Well, Abel," he said, "I would suggest that he's avoiding us. He's probably getting drunk or making his will."

Abel took five or six deliberate steps, paused, and then turned abruptly. "Fine, he's had enough time to drink. Let's go get him."

"What, right now?" the other twin asked. "Just waltz right into the middle of the suburb while people are out washing their scooters and drag the packet chief out of there in cuffs? I've got to hand it to you, Abel. You really know how to handle these delicate jobs."

"Oh, shut up, Zebulon." Abel hiked up his pants and squatted down to pick up a fragment of metal. Then he sent it skating across the loading bay, where it struck a sheet of tin with a bang.

"Settle down," Zebulon said. "We have to stay below the radar on this. If our visit comes up on the list of reports, all we did was a follow-up interview about the packet chief's missing son. We don't want to use unnecessary force. It would be all over the suburb in minutes and show up on the buzz tapes that dump to Central."

"What about the new bugs in his house? Can't we find out what he's doing through them?"

"No. Half of them aren't placed yet, and they need to be tuned. It'll be tomorrow before they transmit data."

"What about the old bugs?"

"Just the auditory ones came up. I can pick up the television, but that's it."

"Well, damn it! What do we do, then? I don't want to sit

around here all afternoon." Abel executed an impatient pirouette and shoved a freight bot out of his way. The massive bot hummed out an apology and rolled off.

"I'll tell you what we do," Zebulon said. "We leave, and we interview the security bot. Maybe we talk to the BNBRX packet chief again. Then we come back tonight. Around one o'clock in the morning, we quietly unlock Walter Earle Glass's front door, and the suburb doesn't see him or his lovely wife Patricia Grace Johnson Glass ever again."

Abel mulled over the plan. "I thought you said we had to stay below the radar. Don't you think a missing packet chief is going to be trouble?"

"We'll put a standard detention order into the system," Zebulon said, "because he skipped this meeting. Then we'll upgrade it to a conviction tomorrow morning and link that to a hiring request. When we detain him tonight, I think he's going to confess that he and his wife helped their son escape."

"How do you know?" Abel asked. "Oh! I get it."

"Exactly. Central still suspects him even though he had a clean lie detector test. They'll probably give us a nice pat on the back. Anyway, packet chiefs aren't important anymore. The new freight bots can run a loading bay by themselves."

"All right," Abel agreed. "But when we get back to Director Montgomery, it's your job to explain why we went to the trouble of planting those bugs today and then didn't wait till we could use them. I don't want the price of forty-five top-of-the-line visual bugs to wind up coming out of my paycheck."

"Fine," said Zebulon, and the two men climbed back into

their packet car. A moment later, alarm bells sounded, and the car chugged out of the bay.

Martin stood up to watch it leave.

"Nasty guys, Chip," he said.

"They certainly are."

Dad was right behind him. "This is it, Tris," he said. "They intend to convict us."

Mom emerged from behind a pallet of air conditioner ducts. "Who'll move into my house? I worked so hard on it!"

Martin's head started to pound. "I thought you two were going to stay back!"

"We have to keep an eye on you," Mom said. "You're just a boy."

Martin decided to ignore this. "Okay, look, they left to go to BNBRX," he said. "We need to leave right now. By the time they get back here tonight, we can be miles away, cross-country, and neither of those losers is gonna risk following us and tearing up his nice white socks."

Dad frowned. "Is something going to happen to our socks?"

"Come on," Martin said to Chip. At least one member of his party had the good sense to do what he said. He went back to fetch his knapsack, slung the pairs of bottles over Chip, and hurried across the loading bay.

The freight bots spotted their packet chief and all began vibrating at once. They clustered around Dad in a tight ring and rolled across the loading bay with him. "Calm down, calm down," Dad told them. "Hush up now. I'm fine. Boys, it looks like you'll be getting a new boss. We did good work here, didn't we?"

Chip stopped on the steel rails and morphed into a small rolling packet car to get them safely past the alarms. His head stayed a dog's head, but his body resembled a playground toy on wheels, with stiff legs and a plank for a back. This time, the plank had notches in it to hold ten large plastic water bottles that dangled from their ropes and sloshed around. The rolling toy was so short, it barely had room enough for Martin.

"What in blazes is that thing?" demanded his father.

"He's not long enough," Martin said in dismay. "It's the water bottles. He's never had so much to carry before." The dog on wheels turned his head toward Martin and rolled his dark eyes apologetically. The caricature of a tail, barely a wisp this time, hung down in shame.

"Are you telling me— Oh, my head! Is that your *Alldog*?"

Mom stopped beside Martin. She extended a tentative hand to touch Chip's fuzzy ears. Then she ran her hand across his board of a back.

"So that's how you got out," she marveled. "Our birthday present!"

"A defective toy? But what about the freight bots?" Dad turned to his faithful crew. "Aren't the freight bots going to do something? Sound the alarm?" He touched his watch. "Call me?"

"No, they like him. Look, we have a problem. I thought Chip could carry us all out at once, but he can't because he's holding the bottles. I'll go first and unload the bottles at the other end, and then I'll send him back for you."

"No, I'll go first," Dad said bravely, "and make sure it's safe." He hesitated. "Is *he* safe?"

"Oh, for crying out loud, Dad, he's just a dog. I have to go first, I'm used to it. He won't have the bottles when he comes back, so you should be okay to ride out together." Before they could argue, he straddled Chip's short board. "See you soon," he called.

Chip rolled through the dim washing room, and water dripped down the back of Martin's shirt. Then came the dark tunnel that seemed to get longer every time they came through it. At last, daylight filtered in through the open end, and Martin prepared to whoop with glee at the sight of the sun. But Chip slammed on the brakes just before the tunnel mouth and refused to budge.

"What's wrong?" Martin asked, scrambling off the load of sloshing bottles.

In answer, Chip softened back into a dog and cowered down on the rails. Martin tiptoed to the edge of the tunnel, crouched down, and peered outside.

The maroon packet car stood on the rails about forty feet away. Its door was ajar, banging in the wind.

"Oh, *crap*!" Martin jerked out of sight and sat down with his back against the tunnel wall. "They *didn't* leave the suburb. They lied! They must have lied because they knew we were listening. What are we gonna do now, Chip? We can't get out!"

CHAPTER FIVE

Chip crept up to Martin, and he smoothed the dog's ears. His hands felt as if he'd held them in ice water, and his fingers weren't working right.

"What are we gonna do?" he whispered. "Okay, calm down, let's think. For starters, I do *not* wanna go back in there and tell Dad and Mom, because Dad's gonna get that look on his face and say, 'I knew this was crazy.' And I don't wanna sit here and wait for them to start rolling that car around, because if they roll it in here, there's not a whole lot of room." And he hastily pulled his legs back from the shiny steel rails. "So that means going out there. Maybe I can figure out what they're up to."

As if in approval, a warm breath of wind curled into the tunnel and brought with it the smell of dirt and growing things. "Yep," Martin said, "that's the right thing to do."

As quickly and quietly as possible, Martin unroped the bottles from Chip and slipped out of his knapsack. Then he slithered forward until the car was in sight again. Nothing about it had changed. Anyone who pushed aside the flapping door would spot him at once.

"That little building over there," Martin whispered, pointing to a metal storage shed twenty feet away. "On my signal. But quiet!" And they scooted out of the tunnel toward the shed. Chip seemed to float like a ghost, without a sound. Martin tiptoed as fast as he could.

Once behind the shed, Martin threw himself down into the

stiff weeds and froze, listening for pursuit. Then he listened for any sound at all. Then he lifted his head and looked for movement.

Nothing met his gaze but plants waving back and forth in their endless dance and a few beetles sedately trekking through the dust. The steel dome rose beside him from its cradle of concrete. It cast its shadow over Martin.

He crawled like a commando for another few yards to the shelter of a big metal hulk. It had many iron wheels running along its sides, a squat body, and a top like a jar lid. From the lid protruded a long thin barrel that looked like it might have been a gun. Martin slithered around the hulk inch by inch, watching for scorpions. Then he peeked out from its shade. A shiny wheel stood on the rails not four feet from him. He was by the back end of the maroon packet car.

"So you let him go," a voice said nearby, and Martin froze like a rabbit. "How does that not violate your programming?"

"I was confident of his safety, sir."

The voices appeared to be coming from inside the packet car. Martin realized he was holding his breath and let it out in a puff. Fur tickled his cheek. Chip had oozed up beside him, his muzzle next to Martin's face.

"That's the security bot's voice," Martin whispered to him. "The freight bot with the big doll's head. That's right! They said they were gonna interrogate him before they left."

"You were confident?" queried the agent's voice. "You said yourself you didn't even see where he went."

"I didn't need to, sir," the security bot answered. "My partner took care of him."

"Your partner? You told us you work alone."

"I do, sir."

"So if you work alone, how could you have a partner?"

"I don't know, sir."

Impatience was palpable in the agent's voice. "Do you realize you're not making a blind bit of sense?"

The bot sounded aggrieved. "You told me to tell you the truth."

"Hold on," interrupted the other twin, and from his confident tone, Martin thought he might be Zebulon. Zebulon seemed to be the one with the ideas. "I think what you're telling us is that, at least for a while, another security bot showed up, one of your own class."

"No, sir," the security bot said. "He wasn't another bot of my class. He was me. Another . . . no, not another . . . a me. My partner was me, because I work alone."

A puzzled silence followed. Martin turned to Chip. "Did that make any sense to you?" he whispered.

"Pardon me, but if you're satisfied now, I need to leave," the bot said. "I have a security matter to attend to. A human is in the yard."

"Yes," Abel said sarcastically. "Two humans. Us!"

"No, sir. Someone else is in the yard."

Uh-oh! thought Martin.

Zebulon spoke. "A human, out here? Really?"

Martin sat up and banged his head against the bottom of the hulk.

Chip pulled himself into a crouch. He didn't vibrate, not exactly, but Martin's hearing on Chip's side went funny.

"Oh, never mind," the security bot said. "My partner has it."

Another silence followed. Then Zebulon's voice said gently, "Your partner. Who is you. Although you work alone."

"Yes, sir." The bot sounded relieved. "I think you've got it now."

"Abel, shove that pile of junk out the door, and let's be on our way. If I was the packet chief around here, I'd write out an order to replace it!"

The security bot landed with a clatter on the gravel railbed. Then the door slammed shut. The maroon packet's engine sputtered to life, and the steel wheels started to turn. Martin lay flat and listened to it chug away into the distance.

"So it's you," the monstrous bot said, gazing at them with reproach in its big blue eyes. "If I'd known it was you, I could have brought you in to talk to them, and maybe then they would have believed me."

"They were just being mean," Martin said as he stood up. "I thought you made all kinds of sense."

The bot gave him a smile and rolled away.

Martin and Chip ran to the mouth of the tunnel. Chip galloped inside while Martin dragged the bottles and knapsack off the rails. A couple of minutes later, Mom and Dad came rolling down the line, looking pale and overwrought.

"Why did you leave us so long?" Mom cried. "I was worried!"

She slid off her makeshift ride and ran to him. Chip had to screech to a stop and stumble sideways to avoid colliding with her, and Dad fell flat on his back on the rails.

"Tris, for crying out loud!" he said.

"I was worried about you," Mom said again as she enveloped

Martin in a hug. Then she looked through the tunnel mouth. "Oh, goodness!"

Martin extricated himself and followed her line of sight: pale sky, a couple of plump white clouds, some dried weeds, little outbuildings, and rusted piles of junk, all bounded by the high cinder-block fence.

"I hate to tell you, Mom, but that's pretty ugly. Save yourself for the good stuff."

He marshaled them along to the outer gate. Mom shaded her eyes as she squinted up at the sky and tripped over rails, rocks, pebbles—everything. Dad maintained a distracted commentary on the pieces of equipment they passed. "See that? That moves earth; you can tell. They must have moved a lot of it to make that access space you showed us."

Then Chip rolled them through the outer gate, and even Dad was speechless.

Martin stood at the top of the hill that fell away for miles into the distance, and joy swelled in his heart. Without the blockade of buildings and fence, the strong wind pushed and shoved at him, and he opened his arms to let it flow past. Ahead, a flock of birds swooped and turned like a single entity, and Mom put her hands over her mouth and started to cry.

"Now, this looks better," Martin told her. "See those? They're blackbirds. And this crazy bot named Hertz told me that the bushes over there with the silver leaves are sagebush. No, sagebrush. Anyway, same thing."

He reached for the water bottles to load Chip up again, but the German shepherd barked happily at him and tore off at a dead run, then came swinging back around like a boomerang.

Martin grabbed for him as he whirled past, and took off running in his wake. "Chip, you moron! Get back here!" he yelled. But it felt good to yell, and good to run, while his parents put their arms around each other and looked at the world in amazement.

Dad cleared his throat and picked up his canvas satchel. "Where did those agents go?" he asked gruffly. "How far do we have to go to get away from them?"

"We can go wherever we want," Martin decided, and the realization made him almost burst with excitement. "Anyplace we wanna go, that's where we're going. All this out here is ours."

Dad looked around. "Where's the fishpond?"

"Okay, fish," Martin said. "We'll go this way, to the mountains. There's a lake there, and I've seen rivers. They've got fish in them."

They started off. Dad kept wiping his eyes.

"I know, Walt," Mom said. "I never imagined a place could be so beautiful."

"It's not that," Dad said, looking embarrassed. "It's just that it's so *bright*."

"Oh, hey," Martin said. "We gotta get you guys covered up! And me, too, even though I'm used to it. Pull out your sheets. Dad, did you bring a sheet or just a blanket? No, not the blanket. Get your sheet."

They helped one another drape the sheets over their heads and shoulders. Martin couldn't help laughing when they were done. Dad was enveloped in brown-and-green plaid, and Mom in pale lilac with blue flowers.

"You look like a ghost, Mom," he said. "A ghost with no fashion sense."

"Well, you look like a laundry pile," she countered. "And now I can't see the view."

They shambled on their way again, hampered by their protective layer. After a while, Dad stopped wiping his eyes, but by then, he was puffing loudly enough to be heard over the wind hissing through the wildflowers.

"Need . . . to stop," he panted. "Pack and tackle . . . too heavy. We can just . . . stay here."

Martin turned around. The dome still loomed behind them, a gigantic steel bubble gleaming fiercely in the midday sun, and he could still make out the line of track that the maroon packet car would travel once the agents' interrogation of Fred was complete.

"We haven't gone very far," he pointed out. "We gotta keep going. We need to get out of sight."

Dad dropped his fishing gear and turned to look back at the dome. Then he mopped the sweat from his face with the corner of his sheet. "You're right," he panted. "Too close."

"Walt, I'm sorry," Mom said, "but I've told you for years you need to get daily exercise. It's very important to lose abdominal fat. All the morning shows say so."

Across their line of march grew a shabby thicket of scrub oak trees with thick, waxy, ugly leaves. They entered the thicket and could no longer walk straight ahead, but had to weave in and out among the rough trunks. Birds swooped across their path or sat on the spindly branches and sang.

"This is good," Martin said. "It'll be harder to find us in here. That should make you happy, Dad."

There was no answer.

Martin turned around and pushed back his sheet so he could see better. "Hey, Dad?" he called. "Mom, we've lost Dad!"

They hurried back the way they had come and soon found Dad. He had sagged down onto a low outcrop of rock. His mouth was open. "Tried to . . . call," he gasped. "Had to . . . sit down."

"Walt!" Mom said. "Walt, goodness! You're so red, you're purple!"

Martin disconnected a water bottle. Dad drank some and made a face. "Already warm," he groaned.

"Look, we need to get going," Martin said, picking up Dad's pack. "I'll carry this if you can get the fishing stuff."

After that, they made good time. Dad sauntered along while Martin struggled with the heavy pack. Martin's temper began to wear thin, but he refused to slow down. He was determined to show Dad up.

By early evening, they came to the bank of a lazy stream about half a foot deep and fifteen feet wide. It flowed over pebbles and orange dirt, cutting tiny channels for itself and leaving narrow sandbars high and dry. Long, curvy patterns in the wet sand seemed to trap the tracks of waves. Tall cotton-woods shaded the little stream, and many delicate bird tracks stippled the shore.

"Let's stay here tonight," Martin said, dropping Dad's pack and rubbing his sore arms. "It looks like a fun place to explore."

"It does," Mom agreed.

Dad unwound himself from his plaid sheet and looked around in vague confusion. "But . . . ," he began.

Martin was easing his own pack from his shoulders. The minor movements this exercise required of his strained limbs felt like the cartilage-popping contortions of a circus athlete.

"But what?" he asked crossly.

"I don't know." Dad lifted his hands. "It's just that there's nothing here."

"We've got water," Mom pointed out. She was folding her stained sheet into a tidy rectangle. "Martin, can we drink it?"

"I've got a filter for it," Martin said.

"But—no house," Dad said, turning to gesture at their surroundings. "No chairs, no beds, no fridge, no cooker, no table, no plates, no nothing. No television, and tonight's the last night of *Chef's Got Game*."

"Are you serious?" Martin cried. "You've got a million great things to check out here, and all you can think about is the stupid television?"

Mom silenced him with a look, and he stomped off. Then she stepped up to Dad and put her arms around his waist. "It's an adventure," she said. "Our first real adventure, Walt. We don't need an easy chair."

"Maybe you don't," Dad said. But he kissed her.

Martin pulled the pairs of bottles off Chip. More than a few were already empty. He took the filter from his pack, found a spot near the bank where the river was deeper than a couple of inches, pushed the hose down into the water, and started to pump. His sore arms immediately protested. The pump took a lot of force. Hertz had made it seem so easy.

Martin wondered for a few uneasy seconds about Hertz. The rugged outdoorsman had seemed normal at first, as if he belonged in the great outdoors. He had known everything about how to survive out here, and yet he was a bot. Where was he now? Were there other bots like him, wandering the hills? Martin pushed the thought away.

Dad came over to see what he was doing. "I'll take a turn, son," he said, reaching for the pump, and Martin's resentment toward him eased.

While they pumped, the heat of the day backed off. Then the birdsong died down. Martin glanced up to find that the glade around them had turned golden, and at that same moment, Mom let out a shriek.

"It's red!" she cried. "It's cherry red! You have to come see this!"

They followed her up a little rise. The sun was setting. Sedately, it gathered its colors in the peaceful western sky. Gold blended into rose, which blended into vermilion, then finally coalesced into the sun's broad crimson ball. The sun withdrew with tremendous dignity before the coming night.

Dad was speechless, and Mom cried.

The clear sky changed almost imperceptibly in the aftermath of the sunset as it faded into twilight. A cool wind flowed over them, the first breath of the chilly night breeze. "You gotta watch for the stars," Martin advised. "One minute, you won't see any, and the next minute, you'll see five or six."

"I think I see one," Mom said.

Dad smacked his own arm. "Hey! Look at that!" The meager light revealed what seemed to be a small black tangle of sewing thread next to a dark smear. "I saw it!" Dad said. "It stuck me with a needle. It took a sample of blood!"

"Oh yeah," Martin said. "It's not a big deal. It's just this weird kind of bug."

"It's a tracking bug," Dad said. "Tracking us. For the agents!"

Mom plucked the delicate tangle from his arm and tried to examine it in the failing light. The stars came out, but she wasn't looking at them anymore.

Martin shook his head. "No, Dad. I've gotten stuck by those lots of times. They just whine around. And those A and Z twins don't even know we're gone yet."

"Not twins," Dad said. "They're clones. All the agents are clones of the same person. I've worked with agents three times, and they look the same, just a little older or younger. 'You know how we took over the Agency?' one of them said to me once. 'We weren't smarter or stronger than the other agents. It's just that we never give up.' They never give up. And now they're tracking us."

Martin started to scoff, but then he didn't. The ice blue stare of Hertz intruded uncomfortably on his thoughts. Hertz, with his built-in killing device. With the radio link back to his masters.

I lost someone very important to me, Hertz had said. But later, he'd told Martin he'd never seen another human being. Had Hertz been placed in the wilderness to track somebody down? Someone he had been programmed to find?

"I can't believe I let you talk us into coming out here," Dad said. He stalked to his backpack, jerked his sheet off the ground, and muffled up in it. "The bugs in the suburb listened to us and watched us, but we didn't have bugs with needles!"

CHAPTER SIX

When Martin awoke in the morning, the sun was already up and birds were starting to flit among the branches. A trail of tiny black ants was taking a shortcut along a fold of his sheet. He sat up to find a thin wild dog the color of gray dust drinking from the bank across the river. It stopped when he moved and stared at him through amber eyes. Then it trotted away.

Mom was working on a watercolor of the tall cottonwoods against the morning sky. "It's amazing how different the colors are out here," she said. "I'm mixing colors I've never used before."

Dad had his pants rolled up, and he was splashing around in the river. Martin thought he was having fun, but Dad waded back to shore with a frown.

"The fish out here are no larger than my little finger," he said. "I don't know why you told me to bring my fishing gear, and I have no idea what we're going to eat."

"This is a tiny river," Martin said. "It's got tiny fish in it. Trust me, they get bigger than that."

They packed up for the hike. Mom was disappointed when Martin made them wrap up in their sheets again.

"Look," Martin said, tucking his sheet securely around him, "you wouldn't even believe what I looked like on my second day. I hurt so much, I thought I was gonna die. You're pink on the nose already. You don't wanna get worse."

They trekked toward the mountains. Dad insisted on

helping to carry his pack, so he and Martin slung it between them, and each held a strap. Martin soon grew to hate this. They had to walk so close together that they made each other stumble, and Martin could no longer pick his own way through the rocks and scratchy weeds.

The ground began to rise and fall in short, steep hills. The higher ground was hard for them to tackle because of the weight of their packs and the burning sunshine, but the gullies between the hills were so choked with short bushy scrub that there was little room to walk.

At their first break, Chip scared up a covey of quail. The birds flew off with such a loud beating of wings that Mom and Dad jumped and gasped, and even Chip sprang back. Martin laughed at them, but Dad grew stern.

"There's danger out here, son," he said. "You may choose not to think about it, but some of us have to."

"I think about it," Martin protested. He had just discovered a wonderful new variety of bug. It lived inside a little cone in the orange sand. It had huge jaws like tweezers, and everywhere it went, it scooted backward on its soft little behind. It was scooting across Martin's hand right now. Martin was completely enchanted with it.

"And what about the wild animals we keep seeing? And those plants with spikes all over them? And what about this sheet? Why do we have to muffle up like children at a costume party? Because the light's trying to kill us, that's why."

"It doesn't *kill* you," Martin pointed out.

Dad ignored him. "I think it's time we faced facts," he said sorrowfully. "This may not be blowing sand and poison gas—although it might have been when the domes were built—but I'm afraid it's just as impossible to live out here the way it is. Our leaders were right about putting us inside domes."

Martin was so angry, he started to shake. He dropped the wonderful new bug back into the ruin of its home. "Our leaders!" he said. "Our leaders were maniacs."

"Martin!" Mom cried.

"They were, Mom. No kidding! They were evil cold-blooded killers. The blowing sand was just a big trick so they could kill off anybody they wanted to."

Dad drew himself up. "That kind of speech is hateful and offensive, particularly coming from a child."

"Walt, it's my fault," Mom said. "When Cassie left, I'll admit I thought horrible things, and I let Martin know about them. But, Martin, you can see now how wrong I was. Even Cassie's school turned out to be true. And if we're in trouble, that's our fault, not the fault of our leaders. We're the ones who broke the rules."

"Martin broke the rules," Dad said. "Son, you're ungrateful. You don't know how lucky we are. Were. How lucky we were."

Martin stood up and looked his parents squarely in the eye.

"Oh, yeah, I do know," he said. "I know exactly how lucky we were. See, way back when, about a hundred years ago, a President got to thinking. 'What do I need all these people for?' he thought, because we were sick a lot, and we needed medicine, and big crowds of us didn't have jobs. So he said, 'I know what I'll do. I'll plan this big epidemic, like everybody's going to die, and I'll get the science people to help me make it look real. And people will be so scared, they'll give up living in this beautiful world and hide under my stupid little domes.'"

Mom put up her hands as if she were pushing his words away. "Oh, Martin, that's wicked!" she said. "How could you make up such a thing?"

"Because I didn't make it up. I got told the whole story. And the guy who told it to me should know, too, because he's a scientist, and he knew all about what the science people did to help. He's the one who stole Cassie and the other Wonder Babies before the government could collect them. He's the reason they've got a school, and he says it'll be really bad if the government ever finds out where they are."

Dad shook his head in disbelief. "So the domes were a fraud? Are you serious?"

"Does this sound like a joke?" Martin said. "The President decided if he only had a few people, he could give them everything he wanted them to have, and everybody around the world would marvel at how great his people were. But before he could get to those great people, first he had to kill off nine hundred and ninety-six people out of every thousand. He only kept four. Four out of every thousand! Now, that's what I call sick."

Dad and Mom looked deeply troubled. Mom kept glancing over her shoulder, as if she suspected some walls might have followed them into the wilderness and be lurking behind a juniper bush, listening. Dad turned away and busied himself with a water bottle. "Anyway, you have no proof," Dad said.

"I kinda wish I didn't," Martin said. "It's not my favorite thing, but I've seen the real, old suburbs, and they cover more ground than we can walk in a day. Every house is ruined, but every one is bigger than ours. And their roads were bigger, and their buildings went way tall, and their grass and flowers weren't just plastic stickers on a window, but plants in a whole square of ground in front of the house, as big as our house back home."

Mom tapped Dad on the shoulder. "That's true," she said in a low voice. "I learned about that from Granny."

"I've seen those flowers, Mom," Martin said. "Big ones. Beautiful. They're still there. Thousands of houses, Dad. Nobody was dying. They were all just fine."

Dad stared at Martin. Then he said the last thing Martin expected to hear.

"Houses."

"What?" Martin said. "What are you talking about?"

"Houses. You said there are houses out here. I want to see them. We need a house of our own."

Martin shook his head. "You don't get it. Those things are worse than a collector bot. I know. I've had to run away from both."

Dad dropped the subject, and they started off again. For half an hour, they toiled up a gradual slope. Once they reached its broad summit, they finally stood above the scrubby growth that had blocked their view of their surroundings for so long. The gray mountains loomed over them now, a daunting spectacle. Dark green pine trees mantled the rounded lower slopes and marched diagonally up the mountains' rocky faces, clinging to long cracks. Behind the nearest peaks, Martin could see more distant, higher peaks, whose cliffs and crags were bare of life.

"We haven't gotten very far," Dad said, disappointed. "HM1 is right over there."

Two or three miles away, a dome caught the full force of the afternoon sun and reflected it toward them in a blinding starburst of light. Martin squinted at the shimmering halo, and then he stood on his tiptoes and squinted to the south. Sure enough, another starburst dazzled him from that direction, high on a hill and far away.

"There's our dome, Dad, way back over there. The dome you're looking at is Fred's suburb, BNBRX."

"How do you know?"

"Because I came past BNBRX twice, on the other side of it. See that short hill on the other side of the dome? You can just see there's something white there; it looks like a big salad bowl when you're next to it. I think it must be Points Visual, where the camera is. That's where the packet lines split too. One line comes to us, one goes to BNBRX, and one goes up north, toward the abandoned suburbs."

Mom shaded her eyes and leaned forward, as if six inches of space would make all the difference in getting a clearer view. "I see the white thing," she said. "I almost think I see the packet line, but that's probably just wishful thinking."

Dad squinted hopelessly. "I don't see a white bowl. So you say the abandoned suburb is ahead? Can you see it? We need to look at those houses."

"It's a *long* way away," Martin said. "Across open country where those agent guys could spot us. There's even a weird bot out there. Chip didn't like him."

That wasn't strictly true. *Hertz* hadn't liked *Chip*; he was the only bot in Martin's experience who hadn't. But that wasn't something Martin felt like thinking about right now.

"Can you see them from here?" Mom asked. "Because I see things that look like houses. Right over there."

She pointed to a patch of thick forest to the north of them, nestled at the feet of the gray mountains. Sure enough, Martin could see the ragged outlines of tumbledown structures poking through the dusty green leaves.

"I can't really tell," he lied. But even Dad could see them.

"Fantastic!" he said. "With any luck, we'll have a front door to close tonight."

Martin tagged after his parents as they headed down the hill. He had goose bumps on his arms.

"Dad, no! Why do we need a front door? We're fine without one."

"I think he's right, Walt," Mom said. "I like sleeping under the stars. It's nice to feel the air moving past our faces."

Dad's expression didn't change.

"We face more kinds of danger out here than I care to count," he said. "The least we can do is go indoors at nightfall."

Martin shivered. "There's things indoors. Way worse things inside than outside."

"Well, we'll just have to see about that."

The yellow blaze of sunset was upon them by the time they reached the edge of the forest that held Dad's houses. Tall shade trees towered above the native scrub. Long shadows stretched across a flat, narrow patch of rock seeded here and there with the hardiest of weeds. Mom mistook it for a dry streambed. Martin was the one who identified it as a road.

Twilight fell as they walked along it. The shade trees bent over them as if they were closing the travelers in. Dad stopped every few feet to peer through the tangle of tall weeds at the road's edge. "Where did those houses go?" he said. "We need to find a place for the night."

"Dad, the last thing we wanna do is spend the night in one of them," Martin said. "Those places, it's like living your own game of Make-a-Mutant Battle Machines House-to-House Hunt-Down."

"You can't equate real life with some silly game," Dad said. "Your mother and I need you to be mature about this."

The first house they found was about fifty feet from the road. The walk to its doorstep was an obstacle course around ancient machinery and old junk, as if a garage sale had spread itself out across the ground and then, lacking visitors, had mummified. Mom got her foot caught in a mesh of twisted wire. Chip lit his eyebeams, and Martin dug out his flashlight so they could figure out how to free her.

"See what I mean?" Martin said, scanning the shadows anxiously. "And we aren't even inside."

They climbed broken steps onto a wide concrete porch. The front door had warped into a saucer and half lay, half leaned in place, holding on to the doorframe by the lower hinge alone. When Dad and Martin tried to maneuver it out of the way, it snapped off the frame with a sound like a gunshot. From the trees came a fluttering and scurrying. From inside the house too.

"Dad, this place is occupied," Martin said desperately.

"Son, I think you need to keep quiet."

Dad set his pack and gear down on the porch. He took Martin's flashlight, walked around the fallen door, and went into the dark house. Dad took two loud, creaky steps. Then his shadowy form vanished in a dull, splintering crunch, and the flashlight went flying through the air.

CHAPTER SEVEN

"Chip! Light!" Martin yelled.

The twin beams of Chip's eyes lit up Dad's face, contorted in terror. His head was where his feet should have been. For one sickening second, Martin thought his father had been decapitated. Then he picked out grimy arms, scrabbling for purchase on the rotten floorboards. The rest of Dad appeared to be gone.

"Floor! Floor!" Dad gasped. Small white insects, like tiny ghosts, flitted across his upper body and disappeared into the rips and gaps of his buttoned shirt.

"Walt!" cried Mom, rushing forward. Chip danced sideways to bodycheck her, and the room fell into darkness again. Martin caught hold of Mom's arm. He heard hoarse rattles as Dad fought for breath.

"Gotta stay here," Martin said. "The floor's gone."

"Oh, Walt!" she cried.

Chip's eyebeams picked Dad out from the shattered floor again. Martin could see the veins standing out on Dad's temples. Dad gurgled and coughed, and one of the white bugs came sailing out of his mouth and landed near Martin's sneaker.

"Chip, can you stretch out long?" Martin asked. "See if you can reach him."

The bot dog crouched down in the doorway and stretched himself out. Two long vines appeared to sprout where his front legs should be. Quickly, they wrapped around Dad at floorboard level, right below the armpits. The boards squeaked loudly in protest as Chip's paws levered Dad loose, and Dad came crawling out over the warped door.

"Good job, Chip!" Martin said, and Chip scrambled up from the doorway to lick his ear.

"Are you all right?" Mom asked. She made Dad sit on the concrete steps. "Let's get those nasty things off you, Walt; they're even in your hair. You've torn your shirt. Oh, there's blood. Martin, we need the first aid cream."

Dad's face was haggard in the light from Chip's eyebeams, and he bled from a dozen scrapes. The knees of his pants had shredded, and the left sleeve of his shirt flopped around his elbow.

"I told you, Dad," Martin said. "You looked just like the little people in David's ImCity game when they stepped on slime demons."

"Martin Revere Glass," said his mother, "this is not a joke!"

"Hey, I'm not the one who called it silly," Martin countered. "Maybe now Dad believes me about these houses."

"He's right, Walt. We were better off by the little river. First thing tomorrow, we're getting out of here."

Dad managed to get to his feet, and they limped away from the deadly structure. But he was too shaken to travel far, and they wound up bedding down in the middle of the stony road. It was by far the most uncomfortable choice they could have made, and the broken house seemed dangerously near. As night fell, it looked more and more like a scene from Martin's monster games. He twisted to and fro on his bedroll, scanning for enemies.

The moon shone its pale beams through the whispering canopy overhead. Small pools of moonlight lapped the weedy ground and picked out and ennobled odd bits of junk in the yard. Dad dozed off, then thrashed as if he were falling through the floor again. His sudden movement startled Martin, and something else, too: a black shape nearby went crashing off into a thicket of young trees.

The oppressive feeling of danger hung over Martin's restless sleep. He could sense the presence of the hideous house brooding over them as they lay side by side on the weedy road. He could feel silent shapes watching them from the bushes. He jerked himself awake and sat up.

Chip was on his feet, barking. Several pairs of eyes caught the light of the moon. Dark forms circled Martin's little camp— three or four at least. Martin couldn't make out what they were, but they were big, bigger than Chip, prowling on four legs and snuffling close to the ground.

Chip's barks had turned into a savage roar. But the glowing eyes refused to retreat. They shifted and winked and drew closer.

Then Chip sprang over Martin, and the eyes rushed to meet him.

Martin couldn't see what happened, but he heard it. He heard crunching and tearing. He heard slobbering, choking breath. And over it all, he heard the sound of Mom sobbing, high and quick, like birdsong.

One of the assailants got away. Its strident yelps of pain diminished in the distance. The other attackers didn't escape. Martin thought he heard weak scrabbling coming from nearby, but the sighing wind drowned it out even as it brought to him the nauseating odor of blood.

Chip came back. Worried growls bubbled out of him, low and muttering, like an old man's mumbled complaints.

"Tris?" That was Dad, very quiet, as if other things might overhear him. But those other things weren't listening anymore. Martin thought he could make out a lump on the dark ground before the evil old house, an addition to the eternal garage sale.

"Walt!" That was Mom, a little breathless, and then the two shadows that were his parents locked together.

"Chip, how are you doing, boy?" he whispered. His hands found Chip's ears in the dark, nervous and pricked, swiveling this way and that. Martin rubbed the soft fur around them.

"Martin, are you all right?" Dad's voice was stronger now.

"Yeah," he said. "I think so. My leg's asleep."

"Is the bot all right?"

"He's just a little upset right now."

"Martin . . . are you sure that thing is safe?"

Chip tucked his big head into Martin's chest, and his growls changed to whimpers.

"If you mean, did he save our lives just now, then yeah, I guess he's safe."

Mom's hand reached out of the darkness to pat Chip's ruff. "Good dog," she murmured.

They got no more sleep that night. At Dad's suggestion, they sat back-to-back in order to keep watch in all directions. Chip sat up between Mom and Martin, snuffling the breeze to scent for enemies.

Daylight brought a grisly scene and a loud buzzing of flies. Three huge dogs lay sprawled among the weeds and junk in front of the evil house. They had very short, smooth black-and-tan coats that revealed their bulky muscles and lean flanks. All three were bigger than Chip.

Strange injuries marked them. One had a long rip in its hide from breastbone to tail, as if someone had pulled on its zipper. Inside the tear was dark, greasy flesh. Another lay with its head turned around to face its tail, its round white eyes bulging out of its sockets in the manner of a tasteless joke.

"Would you look at that!" Dad marveled.

Chip wouldn't. He didn't come near the dead dogs. He skulked on the opposite side of the road, head and tail drooping. "Come here," Martin coaxed. "You were a good dog. You should be proud."

But Chip was anything but proud.

"They would have killed us," Mom said in a low voice. "Isn't that right? We'd be looking like this right now."

Dad cleared his throat. "Maybe," he said in a matter-of-fact tone, as if she'd asked for his opinion about a fishing tournament. "But my sense is that dogs wouldn't kill in quite this fashion. More bite marks. More tearing, I think. Something that looked . . . more like steak."

Martin's stomach churned. The dead bodies, with their glazed eyes staring into infinity, seemed invested with a horrible power and knowledge.

"Okay, let's get out of here," he said. "I say we head back the way we came. There was this great lake back there, I saw it on my first night out, we must have gone right by it and not known it. It had birds all over it. Big ones. I bet that means big fish, too."

"No," Mom said, and her voice was unusually stern. "No, Martin, your father's right. We aren't safe out here with these wild animals roaming around. We need a front door of our own."

Martin's jaw dropped. "Mom!"

"I'll tell you what we do, Tris," Dad said. "We'll investigate every single one of these old houses until we find a place that's fit for us to live. We're putting walls between us and them, and that's a promise."

CHAPTER EIGHT

Trailing behind his parents as they hiked down the old road, Martin tried to talk them out of their decision. Instead of nagging or whining, he tried honesty: he attempted to convey some idea of the dangerous enemies these houses held. But honesty failed in spectacular fashion. He wasn't surprised. It usually did.

Decayed houses crowded the underbrush at the edge of the road like grotesque monsters shambling into the light. Their busted doors seemed to leer at Martin; the sunlight glittering on their broken windows winked with obscene meaning. The roof of the house closest to him had fallen in, so that it looked like it was wearing a hat pulled down over one eye. "I swear, I've seen zombies hiding in better-looking houses than these," he told them. "We're gonna be sorry once it gets to be night."

Dad ignored him. He sized up the line of sinister wooden buildings as briskly as if they were new scooters. "We won't go look at that one," he said, pointing. "Too worn. It's gone all soft."

"Walt, this one coming up doesn't look so bad."

"Great, Mom," Martin groaned. "That one looks just like our house back home . . . in a few million years, maybe."

Their shabby road wound around the base of a steep, forested hill. Other roads branched off it. Dozens of ruined houses came into view. "Wonderful," Martin whispered. "A whole zombie suburb."

They came around a long curve, and the road changed. It split into two roads running parallel to each other, with a strip of tall weeds and bushes between them. The concrete slabs of the two roads heaved and tilted at awkward angles.

Enormous trees lined each side of the new double road. A number of them were hollow black shells with only a spray or two of green leaves to show that they still lived. Others were dead, rattling skeletons with brittle branches. Several had fallen across the roadway.

Off to the left was open ground, a break from the dilapidated houses. Iron swing set frames and the remains of a stand of bleachers stood among bushes and wildflowers.

"That was a park," Mom said.

A couple of hundred yards beyond the old bleachers, the ground lapped up to the edge of a steep incline covered with massive pine trees. Directly above that slope rose gray granite cliffs.

"Wow!" Martin said. "The mountain starts right over there." The nearness and hugeness of it made his pulse race with excitement. It was accessible. It was personal. Heck, it was part of a park! What fun he and David would have had if they'd had a mountain in their park.

"A park is good news," Dad opined. "The best houses are by the park."

A shallow, pebbly stream flowed down from beneath the dark pine trees at the mountain's foot and cut across the park parallel to their street. It sang loudly with its own importance.

"Come on, Chip," Martin called, and they hurried over to investigate.

The stream wasn't deeper than two or three feet. Its stream-bed was full of light gray rocks, and it foamed over these minor obstacles with great excitement, as if it were a fearsome cataract. Martin liked it right away.

Chip liked it too. He waded into it up to his hocks, and it tried to sweep his tail downstream. He bit at the water while Martin plunked stones into it. Then the two of them ran back to make their report.

"I saw fish, Dad. They were brown, maybe this big, with little spots all over them. Even though the water's moving really fast, they didn't move."

"That's some good news at last."

"Look at that," Mom said. "Over there."

Across from the park, grand houses were set far back from the street, all but invisible beneath tough gray-green vines. Handsome details peeked through the leaves: stately pillars on either side of the driveway, a bay window here, a carved lintel there. They were like nothing Martin had seen before.

"Maybe families were bigger then," Dad said. "I think you could fit twenty people in that one."

Chip sniffed at a statue of a little boy tilted at an angle next to the street. Its stone skin was green with mold, and ivy smothered it; only the head and one chubby arm escaped. Under a massive tree were the concrete ends of what had been a graceful bench. Its boards were gone, leaving only the suggestion of leisure: the ghost of a seat.

"It's cool," Martin said, "but spooky. I like the park better."

They investigated the larger houses as the day wore on. Several of the buildings were promising, but others, being bigger, had just fallen into more dramatic decay. Entire walls of glass had shattered and exposed their rooms to the elements, and massive beams were wedged precariously against shifting supports.

Evening came early in the lee of the towering mountain. A hush had already fallen under the cool shadows of the trees. Birds sang quiet, senseless songs in the lush, overgrown bushes. Even the loud stream in the park sounded subdued now. It had wandered away, and a portion of its water had been diverted into a large, quiet pond.

Martin began to look over his shoulder.

"House-to-House has green skeletons that shoot spells," he said. "During the day, they're these thin, stripy shadows, and at night they glow. But when it's in between, like now, they blend right in with the backgrounds."

Dad was walking a few feet ahead of them. He let out a shout.

"Look at that roof! And almost all the windows are in. A crack here and there, but they'll still do their job."

"The back could be gone," Mom warned before Dad could get too excited, but she had to agree that the house he had found seemed remarkable. Its rows of dark gray shingles were so regular and even, they might have been brand-new. The walls showed no sign of damage either, and no wonder, Martin thought. They were made out of mortared stones.

The house was not as large as the grand wrecks they had already visited, but it wore an air of stately dignity. Two stories tall and wide across the front, it had crisp, clean lines that reassured the eye. The front door was in the exact middle, tucked away behind an arched portico that rested on thin columns. At least, it appeared to rest on them. Martin realized as they walked past it that the left-hand column no longer touched the ground.

"It's a very simple shape," Mom said. "A rectangle. But that's what gives it its beauty."

"It looks like a shoebox," Martin said.

Dad climbed up onto a garden wall that abutted the corner of the house. "This roof is made out of stone. Stone!" he marveled. "That's got to weigh a ton!"

They walked all the way around it. Only a couple of windows were broken. "I can't see in," Mom said, pushing her way between rangy shrubs. "There's a covering on the windows. Some sort of privacy film."

The veneer had peeled off the front door in ugly flakes, but it still stood firm in its hinges. Dad stepped gingerly across a sloping vegetable heap that had built up against the door. Then he rattled the handle.

"It's locked or stuck," he said. "No surprise there. Martin, can your bot give it a try?"

Inside, there was no color. Everything was the gray hue of dust. It furred the banister of the stairwell that faced them and lay like a carpet on its treads. It obliterated the pattern of the hall floor, so that it was impossible to guess what kind of floor it was. And in every beam of dusky light that peeked through the grimy windows, dust motes danced in a hypnotic swirl.

"That's your privacy film," Dad said as they stepped inside, pointing to the dust on the windows.

His voice sent a storm of specks rising, like a flock of pale, infinitesimally tiny birds. In an instant, the air was thick with dust, too thick to breathe. The three of them choked and hacked, and they pulled their sheets up over their noses and spoke in desperate signals to one another. They made their way past the stairs and practically fell into the room beyond, wheezing and gasping.

This room was a little less dusty, but much dirtier. Puffs of air filtering through a couple of cracked panes had kept the dust from forming faery drifts, but brown pellets and droppings ran in trails around the edges of the room, and spiderwebs muffled every object in untidy mummy wrappings. Living spiders still pursued their occupation in the gritty nets alongside the remains of their ancestors. Hollowed-out bodies of insects lay in the caked dirt on the windowsills like carcasses after Armageddon.

Like an optical illusion that turns from a vase into two faces, the dim room suddenly made sense to Martin. It was a living room, and this disreputable object taking up an inordinate amount of floor space turned out to be a very long couch. Here were two chairs beside it; they had probably not always been greasy beige. More objects asserted themselves: an end table, a round table, straight-backed chairs, a lamp. Long draperies of no particular color still hung at the edges of the windows, torn into lacy scoops and scallops by their own meager weight.

"It's so dirty!" Mom gasped once she could speak again.

Dad cleared his throat three or four times. "You've been sleeping on dirt."

The kitchen was bright with windows in spite of the clinging grime. Dried plants in pots lined the window over the sink. Dad pointed out a fridge, but they lacked the fortitude to open it.

Chip found two small dishes on the floor and stuck his nose into them. Small painted paw prints lined their dusty rims.

"Hey, Chip," Martin said. "This is a pet-friendly house. They set out a plate for you."

Dad went to one of the windows and rubbed a clean spot on the glass. "You can just get a glimpse of the park," he said. "Here we are, Tris, another house on the street by the park, and I can't see the fishpond, but I know it's right over there. We'll sleep safe indoors tonight. No more waking up to killer dogs."

Martin's heart sank. After the wide horizons of the outside world, he mistrusted the close space. "I'm gonna look around a little," he said, backing away.

"Don't go up the stairs," Dad said. "The floor up there might not be safe."

This whole place might not be safe, Martin thought.

He held his breath and tiptoed by the front door. The dust storm had not yet subsided. Covering his nose, he hurried down the hall. In this part of the house, cracks in the glass had prevented the dust buildup, and he could explore at leisure.

At the end of the passage, he found the largest bedroom he'd ever seen, a dim, cavernous room with heavy, thick drapes over the windows. These still held together, although Martin suspected that they would tear like paper if touched.

A bad smell hung in the room, acrid and rank, and the bed looked strangely disordered. As they walked past, small squeaks rose from its rents and fissures, and tiny gray mice raced past their feet.

Chip wrinkled his black muzzle at the smell and eyed Martin unhappily.

"No, don't worry," Martin said. "I don't want you to catch one."

A room next to the bedroom was lined with dark objects on shelves, and a padded chair stood before a wide wooden desk. Nothing squeaked or scurried, and here at least the faded brown color scheme seemed to work. The room wasn't dim, but it wasn't bright, either. Bushes or vines had grown up to shade most of the window.

Martin approached the desk to see if the square things stacked on it might be antique game cartridges. A basket on the desk held a mound of pale fur, and a dirty glove lay across it. That seemed like a strange place to leave a glove.

Martin's eye followed glove to sleeve, sleeve to chair. He discovered that the chair wasn't padded after all, but something padded was in the chair. He took two steps to its other side and almost fainted from fright. A skull rested its bony cheek against the desk and surveyed him through wire-rimmed glasses.

The skull and desk wavered. Then they whisked out of sight. The kitchen appeared almost instantaneously. Martin's feet had taken action on their own.

"Skeleton!" he shouted. "Zombie, skeleton!"

Mom and Dad turned toward him, startled.

"Skeleton, skull," Martin babbled. "Skull and glasses—gold teeth! And crap, crap, crap, that wasn't a glove. It was a—a—not a glove!"

"Don't say 'crap,'" Mom said automatically.

Dad said, "Settle down."

Martin became aware that he was dancing from foot to foot, but when he tried to stop, his feet wouldn't obey. "Aren't you listening?" he cried. "There's a skeleton in here, or a zombie or something, just like in House-to-House Hunt-Down! We need to get out before it comes after us. We need to get our hands on a gun!"

"Walt, is it dangerous?" Mom asked.

"I'll go see," Dad said. "Um . . . Chip? Martin, would you ask your bot to come along?"

Dad and Chip left. After a few seconds, Mom followed them. Martin stayed in the kitchen, hyperventilating.

"It's just a dead body," Dad said as he returned. "If your story about the creation of the domed suburbs is correct, it's probably the person who owned this house."

"How do you know that?" challenged Martin in a panic. "Maybe it moved in after the owner left!"

"Ugh," Mom said, making a face as she walked in. "Walt, won't that thing spread disease?"

"I doubt it," Dad said. "Considering the state he's in, I doubt he's any more of a health risk than the rest of this mess. We have plenty of space here. We just won't use that room."

Martin was aghast. "You mean we're gonna sleep in a house with a *skeleton*?"

"It's just a bunch of bones," Mom said. "Trash, like chicken bones. Outside those violent games of yours, skeletons don't walk around."

Dad and Mom went back to the kitchen cabinets. Inevitably, Martin wandered back to the skeleton. He went to the room where it sat and watched it for a while from the doorway. It didn't look like a padded chair at all. Then again, it didn't look like a person in a chair either.

He tiptoed closer, staying out of sight of those grime-filmed spectacles. The back of the skull was hidden by hair, or maybe a mixture of spiderwebs and dust. Inside the wide gap of the shirt collar, the neck had shriveled down to almost nothing, and the whole bony form seemed shrunken, like a boy in his dad's suit.

Martin couldn't make up his mind about it. One second, it seemed small and pitiful. The next, it seemed uncanny and horribly inhuman, and he wanted to smash it with the nearest heavy object he could find.

Rudy had told him that the people who hadn't gotten picked for the domed suburbs lined up to be given euthanasia shots. This was such a big place, with so many houses and so many people. Those lines must have been pretty long.

"I guess I'd want to die at home too," Martin murmured to Chip. "You know, have a little peace and quiet."

The skeleton didn't acknowledge that he had spoken. It continued to slump in the same discolored heap it had formed for decades. Martin plucked up the courage to come closer.

Dry brown skin encased the bony hand in a glove of its own making. It lay in that flattish nest of fur that was piled up in the basket. A pet basket to match the little paw print bowls in the kitchen. A cat bed. The pale fur belonged to a cat.

A vision wove itself together in Martin's mind of the house before the dust, when the neat row of potted plants in the kitchen had been green and flourishing. The world was ending, and people were forming long lines to get their shot. But this man with the paw print bowls couldn't do that. What would happen to his cat? He couldn't just put her outside and not come back. He loved her too much. So he gave his cat poison and stroked her until she lay still, and then he took poison himself. And the soft fur of his cat was the last thing he felt as he drifted away into death.

Martin's throat ached. He knelt down and buried his face in his dog's shaggy fur. "I wouldn't leave you, either, Chip," he said. "Not ever."

Then he walked out of the room without looking back. The skeleton didn't scare him anymore.

CHAPTER NINE

Mom and Dad gathered bundles of grass and tried to sweep out part of the living room so they wouldn't have to lie down in filth. But the spiderwebs stuck to everything and then stuck to them. "Baths for everyone in the pond tomorrow," Mom said with a sigh.

As the sun went down, Mom and Dad congratulated each other on their safety while Martin lay on his bedroll and fretted. He missed the gradual change of light. He could see almost nothing through the dirty windows. The air inside the house was stale and rank, and he missed looking up and seeing the stars. The darker it grew, the more he thought about the skeleton. It wasn't a monster, but it was still a person: the Owner. And maybe the Owner didn't want them in his house.

In the morning, Mom sent Dad and Martin to wash in the pond. "Just us guys," Dad said with a sheepish grin. Martin wasn't keen on the idea, and he was completely unprepared for how ridiculous his father looked without clothes. He lunged into the water to distract himself, and then he lunged back out again. He'd eaten ice cream warmer than that pond.

They hauled ancient trash out of the house all day, until the backyard looked like a dump. Then, when the shadows lengthened across the park, they went to the pond to wash their hands and eat their energy bars.

"If only the cooker worked!" Mom lamented.

"I've checked the attachments," Dad said, shaking his head. "There doesn't seem to be a food delivery chute."

"If only the toilets worked," she murmured next. They silently agreed.

Dad went back into the house and returned with his fishing equipment. No sooner had he cast the line than it took off on a journey. "Got one!" he yelled.

Dad's fish was bigger than the one Hertz had caught. Dad had to hold it with both hands. Its coloring was beautiful, light bronze with dark brown speckles, and its lower jaw stuck out past its upper jaw as if it still wanted to fight, even though Dad had bashed its head on the ground.

None of them knew what to do with it.

"Tris?" Dad said. "Did your cake classes teach you something about this?"

"I know you pull the guts out," Martin said. That had made a big impression on him.

While his parents conferred, Martin wandered away with Chip to explore the perimeter of the pond. They found a large brown frog with dark golden eyes sitting in the muck and a graceful cotillion of blue damselflies skimming above the surface of the water. Martin threw a few rocks in and stood amazed as one of them bounced a couple of times before sinking.

A shout from Dad brought him back up the shoreline. In his absence, they had dealt with the fish.

"How are we supposed to eat this?" Dad demanded. "Is this your idea of a joke?"

Martin eyed the sawed-up carcass. They had tried without

success to remove its skin and had scarified its speckles quite badly. Martin was reminded of the time he'd slid into home plate in shorts and skinned up both his legs.

"Hertz cooked his over a little fire thingy in a pan. I've got his pan in my knapsack."

Dad made them build the fire right next to the edge of the pond on ground that was thoroughly waterlogged. "We don't want this thing getting out of hand," he said.

Martin didn't think the pitiful, inch-high flames were likely to get out of hand. They were much more likely to expire without warning, and they did just that six or seven times before Dad had a fire that was big enough to heat up the pan.

The cooked fish was a sadder specimen than the raw fish had been. Scorched in parts and raw in others, it looked like the victim of a terrible accident. Dad salted it with Hertz's tiny shaker, a hopeless gesture as far as Martin was concerned.

"You can have mine," Martin volunteered.

At this, Dad appeared to burst into flames himself. "You will eat your share!"

So Martin had to take a bite of the fish. It was tough and smoky, but to his surprise, it tasted pretty good. Encouraged by Martin's success, Mom took the fork. "That turned out better than I thought," she said.

"It's edible," Dad agreed, and the lines in his forehead smoothed out. "We've learned some important lessons. Move it around to keep it from sticking to the pan . . ."

"And watch those flames in the middle . . ."

Martin escaped while his parents traded cooking tips.

In the morning, Dad headed out to fish right after breakfast.

"Stay and help your mother," he ordered. "There's lots of cleaning to do."

"Not again!" Martin protested. "I was stuck inside all day yesterday, cleaning stuff. Why can't I go fishing too?"

"You don't know how. Look, son, I'm not doing this because it's fun. I'm doing it because we need food." And, whistling happily, Dad left the house.

Mom told Martin to go around the rooms with a stick, pulling down spiderwebs. Martin dawdled through the kitchen, experimenting with the tensile strength of the dusty nets. If he pulled fast, the web broke and deposited a shower of dried bug parts on his head. If he pulled slowly, the web stretched longer and longer while its living inhabitants scurried for safety. He wandered out to the front hall, more or less expunging webs along the way; tiptoed by the closed door where the Owner had his residence; and entered the master bedroom, no longer gloomy now that its thick draperies were gone, but still foul-smelling from the remains of all the mice who had lived for generations in the shelter of the mattress. When he and Dad had tried to move the mattress, it had fallen into lumps, and they had had to shovel it out with flat boards.

On a shelf in the closet, Martin found a very handsome watch and polished its crystal against his jeans. "Maybe we should take it to the Owner," he said to Chip. "Now that we've found it, giving it back seems like the right thing to do." And he and his dog tiptoed to the Owner's room and left the watch outside the closed door.

They returned to the bedroom. Chip scared up a bewildered mouse and chased it into the closet, and Martin found a dressing table with old bottles of perfume on it. "Check out this bowl, Chip," he said.

He picked up the little bowl from the table and rubbed on his jeans one of the glass decorations it held. It rewarded him with a glow of brilliant color. Each of the six pieces was glass formed to look like candy: bright, colorful disks with twisted glass ends. And when he scraped some of the grime from the bowl itself, a gleam like a rainbow shone through the gray.

"Wow!" he said. "This is the most amazing thing I've ever seen. It's like somebody caught a circus and put it in glass. Let's take it all to the pond and wash off the dirt."

They started down the hall, but Martin stopped when he saw the watch he'd propped by the Owner's door.

"What if he wants this, too?" he whispered to Chip.

He stood for a few seconds outside the closed door behind which the skeleton slumped. This was something he wanted to keep, but if he did, what might be the cost? Shriveled fingers around his neck in the middle of the night?

"Mom," he called. "Mom!"

Mom stood on a chair in the living room, scrubbing the windows with a tattered rag. Martin paused, surprised. The room looked pretty good. Not clean, but at least he could see through a couple of the windows now, and the rotted couch and armchairs were gone.

"What's up?" she asked.

"Mom, what do you think the Owner thinks about us in his house?"

"The Owner?" Mom asked. "Wait. Do you mean the dead body?"

Martin nodded. "Because it's his house. And he's still here."

Mom climbed down from her chair and dunked her rag in a pot of nasty water. Then she wrung it out. "No, he just left his body behind. Like"—she stopped to think—"like old clothes."

"Where did he go, then?" Martin asked.

"Nowhere. He just stopped." She climbed onto her chair and went back to work.

Martin tried to wrap his mind around the concept of stopping. It felt wrong. It felt cosmically unfair. The Owner had loved his cat, taken care of his watch, and selected for his enjoyment a riotously colored dish of glass candy, all actions that Martin thoroughly approved of. The man, once dead, should not have to vanish into chartless oblivion. Martin refused to allow it.

"How do you know that?" he challenged. "How do you know he just stopped? It isn't right. I don't think he did."

Mom paused in the act of swabbing her window. "I guess I don't know," she admitted.

"So he went somewhere," Martin decided. "Somewhere else. Somewhere nice. A place where he doesn't need his body anymore."

"Maybe," Mom said. "I don't see how, but it doesn't matter."

"Yes, it does," Martin said, realizing in dismay that he had argued himself around to his original problem. "Because if he's somewhere else, maybe he comes here every now and then; you know, to visit his favorite things. And then maybe he's gonna be mad at us—you know, if we move them around or take them and stuff."

Mom turned to look at his serious face. Then she climbed off her chair and sat down on it to think. "Oh, I wish I had a green tea soda right now," she sighed. "Okay. I don't know much about being dead, but I do know this. Dead people don't come back to visit their favorite things."

"How do you know?" Martin asked.

"Because Granny didn't come back to visit you, and you were her favorite thing in the world."

Martin's spirits lifted. "Yeah, that's right," he said. "I used to hope she'd come back, but she didn't."

"So did I," Mom said. "For a while."

"Then the Owner won't be back here, either?"

Mom looked at the room, with its end tables but no couch or armchairs and its two clean windows and three horrendous ones. Assiduous sweeping with bundles of weeds had revealed a floor of sunny caramel-colored tiles.

"No, he won't. This house is ours now. I just wish I could figure out how to get a new sofa."

So Martin ran down the slope and across the tree-lined street to wash off his treasure in the pond. The glass candy was larger than life, and bolder, too. One piece was ringed with stripes of cobalt blue and lemon yellow. It had bright blue twists at the ends. One had orange ends and a cherry-colored center that turned the landscape crimson when he looked through it. Another was green glass swirled with what Martin swore were flecks of pure gold.

But best of all was the bowl itself. Dozens of small, round, frilly glass blossoms of every conceivable color crowded together beneath a layer of thick, clear glass. They looked like nothing he had seen before. They looked like flowers in an underwater garden.

Martin could only stare at the bowl. He knew no words ornate enough to describe its beauty. Beside him, Chip's rapt expression mirrored his own.

"*Martin!*"

Dad was stomping down the pond bank toward them, his face puffy with anger. "Stop ignoring me! What are you doing here? You're scaring the fish!"

"Nothing. Just . . . nothing." Martin instinctively curled his hands around his precious find.

"Then get back to the house and get to work. You've got cleaning to do." And Dad stalked off down the muddy shoreline.

Martin ran back to the house.

"Don't slam the door," Mom called reproachfully. "You're scattering the dust."

Martin stashed his beautiful bowl in a kitchen cabinet and then burst into the room where she was cleaning.

"I hate this!" he yelled. "I never wanted him to come here. We'd be doing great without him; you'd be painting pictures and stuff, and I'd be learning great things about new bugs. But look, he's got us all scared just like he is, and stuck in another house, wiping counters and looking at everything through a bunch of dirty windows." Anger swelled inside him, all his rage over Dad sending Martin's little sister away to die. "I hate him! I do. I wish he hadn't come."

Mom stood still, looking away from him. She said, "I don't know why you'd say such a thing about your father."

I know why, Martin thought. I know a whole packet car full of reasons why. I could tell you why, and then you'd hate him too.

"All I can say," Mom went on, "is that if your father weren't here, I don't think I could stand it. Maybe you'd be having the time of your life, but I would be very unhappy."

Martin ran out of the house and slammed the door again. He noticed that Chip caught it with a back foot to keep it from making a noise, and for a second, his quarrel even extended to his dog. Dad was taking it easy on the bank, slowly reeling in an empty line. Martin charged up to him, and the surprise on Dad's face must have equaled the fury on his.

"She doesn't know!" Martin shouted. "She thinks you're so great, taking care of us and all, but that's only because she doesn't know. I could tell her, and then she'd hate you too. And it would serve you right!"

"Know what?"

Dad's face looked pinched and cautious and silly, like the old man he would be one day, like the ridiculous spectacle he was without his clothes on. Martin felt slimy all over. He threw himself down on the bank next to Dad's tackle box and wanted to cry.

"She doesn't know you thought you were helping the recall when you sent Cassie away."

A full minute went by, while Martin stared at the wide, dark pond and listened to the *whiz-whiz* sound of Dad's reel. The pond was a flat sheet on top, neat and tidy, but who knew what ugliness lay underneath.

"Yes, she does," Dad said at last.

"No, she doesn't!" Martin snapped. "You wouldn't tell her. Even I haven't told her, though I don't know why, except that I just don't want her to know."

"Your mom's not stupid, son."

Dad reeled in his lure, which looked to Martin's untrained eye like a tiny fish with enough hooks dangling from its mid-section and tail to catch about six fish at once. If a creature were dumb enough to bite that thing, it deserved to end up in a pan. Dad paid out line, brought his pole back, and sent the dangerous little fish skimming out across the water.

"What you have to understand," Dad said, "is that I couldn't do a thing about your sister. The recall notice came out, and there it was. The inspection was about to start. There was nowhere I could put Cassie to keep her safe, and Central always gets what they want."

"You could have tried," Martin muttered. He buried his hands in Chip's thick, harsh fur and laid his hot face against his dog's velvet forehead.

Dad glanced over his shoulder, a habit based on a lifetime of cowardice. Martin wanted to laugh at the absurdity of it, but the pit of his stomach hurt.

"If I had moved Cassie out of her routine, your mother would have wanted to know why," Dad said. "If she knew why, she would have fought to keep Cassie by every means she could think of. That wouldn't have worked, and I would have lost them both."

Martin flicked a pebble into the water and watched it sink. "So you chose Mom over Cassie."

"No!" Dad's voice was loud enough to scare any nearby fish. "I couldn't do a thing about Cassie. I didn't choose between them. I just chose not to lose your mother, that's all." He choked, then cleared his throat. "Do you think I wanted that to happen to Cassie? She was my little girl."

Martin remembered Dad coming home and looking at them all, dragging his feet like a very old man. That was the night the recall notice must have come out, the night he had found out Cassie was doomed.

"I don't believe you," Martin said, and his voice was tight. "I don't believe there was nothing you could do. You could have tried. You never know till you try. There's always something to do."

"That's good, son. I don't want you to believe me. I don't want you to know what it's like to feel that you've run out of options."

Martin watched him reel and cast, and then reel and cast again. "So Mom knows?" he said.

Dad blew his breath out in a long, quavering sigh. "Yes. As soon as the recall vote came up, she knew. I didn't have to tell her. She really hated me there for a few days, but I didn't mind. I pretty much hated myself. I was worried about what she might do to herself with you and Cassie both gone. Your mother lives for you kids, you know."

"Yeah," Martin said.

"So Cassie's really fine?" Dad asked. "You didn't just make that up? I . . . well, maybe I don't deserve it, but I need to know."

"Cassie's doing great," Martin muttered. "She's having a great time at the school. Those kids finally have teachers smarter than them. I don't have to make things up," he added with a touch of scorn.

"And . . . does she know about me? About what I did?"

Martin glanced up. Dad's face had that pinched, silly look on it again, the one that made Martin want to cry.

"Nah, I didn't tell her. She thinks you're her hero, talking the parents into sending her off to school. I guess a little kid like her still needs heroes."

Dad nodded. "Even if they're not real."

Martin didn't know what else to say. He opened Dad's tackle box and examined the lures while Dad went on casting and reeling. "How's the fishing?" Martin asked after a while.

"Not so good," Dad admitted. "It's the wrong time of day, maybe. I'll try a few more tricks and call it quits."

"Well, I guess I'll head on back," Martin said, "and, you know, go help Mom."

Dad glanced at his watch. "I'll be along in a few minutes. We'll have an early lunch."

Martin headed up the hill to the house. He wasn't sure how he felt. More than anything else, he felt sad and embarrassed, as if Dad's weakness were part of him now. Dad's crime had become his because he couldn't condemn it anymore. He was an accomplice. Guilt by understanding.

But our house isn't so bad, he thought as he tromped through the weeds in the front yard. I like that it looks like a shoebox. And David and Matt would be so jealous if they knew we had a house with our very own skeleton.

A sweeping session with bundled twigs had cleared the faery dust out of the entryway and revealed a floor of black-and-white marble tiles. "Look, Chip," he said, pointing them out. "That's almost as nice as the factory."

A second later, he came charging down the hill again, with Chip howling behind him.

"Dad! Dad!" he yelled. "Something's wrong with Mom!"

CHAPTER TEN

Mom lay on the caramel-colored tiles of the sunny living room. Dad knelt beside her while Martin ran to the kitchen to bring her a water bottle.

"Thanks," she said, taking a sip. "I'm fine. Don't worry."

"What happened?" Dad asked. "Martin, did you see what happened?"

"She fell," Martin said.

"I feel fine. Just a little dizzy." Mom waved Martin back. "Stop hovering! I'm not made of glass. Get out of the way so I can get up."

Mom clutched Dad's arm as she got to her feet and cautiously released her grip. "There. See? I told you I was fine."

Dad's face lit up in relief. "You don't hurt anywhere? Why don't you sit down? You've been working too hard. Not enough water, maybe that fish from last night . . ."

Mom took two steps and fell headlong with a cry. Chip let out a howl.

"See?" Martin said. "That's just what happened before!"

Dad shoved Chip aside as he threw himself onto his knees. "Martin, would you get that dumb dog out of here?"

Mom lay with her eyes closed. After a few seconds, they opened. "What am I doing down here?"

"You fell," Martin told her.

"Tris, can you remember if you hit your head?"

"I'm fine," Mom said with a trace of irritation this time.

"Really, you two!" She climbed awkwardly to her feet.

This time, Dad caught her when she fell.

"Shut that dog up! Martin, grab your bedroll. Hurry! She's heavy."

"I heard that," Mom said.

Dad lowered her onto the bedroll and helped Martin prop her head up on a folded sheet. "This time, Tris, you need to stay there."

Mom blinked at their anxious faces. "Maybe I am tired," she conceded. "I haven't been getting much sleep."

"Martin, let's let your mother get some rest. Tris, you take a little nap."

Dad escorted Martin and Chip through the front door. Then he shut it and sank down on the front steps. Martin was astonished at the change that had come over his father. Dad seemed to have aged several years.

"Ten minutes after," Dad said. Then he couldn't go on. Tears rolled down his cheeks and got caught in the stubble that had formed there.

Martin was appalled. Mom cried, sure. But Dad?

"After—after—" Martin stammered. "After what?"

Dad wiped his eyes and pointed at his watch. "It's five after eleven, ten minutes after the time when we left the suburb and cleared that last fence. Four days and ten minutes, and she's been sick for about ten minutes. She's not sick. They've disabled her somehow."

This sank in, and Martin collapsed onto the step beside Dad. Chip didn't try to lick his face or beg for pets. The dog looked just as shocked as he was.

"So it's a suburb thing?" Martin ventured.

"Suburb or agents or something like that. I don't know how. I've never heard of such a thing. Why didn't it happen to me instead? Why didn't it happen to all of us?" Dad blew out a breath and rubbed his eyes. "I don't know what to do."

"Are they coming, then?" Martin asked.

"If we're lucky," Dad said in a gruff voice. "If we're lucky, they're on their way. Otherwise, your mother probably just stays . . . just like that. We won't be able to turn it off."

Martin was silent. Nothing this horrible had ever even entered his mind before. He rubbed his hands on the knees of his jeans faster and faster. Chip stuck his nose in the way to force him to stop.

"We never should have come here," Dad groaned. "I never should have allowed it. The game shows aren't that bad. They're humane. We'd be well fed and kept in nice accommodations, and given facials and haircuts and new clothes. Before you die, you're a television star. You're treated with respect."

Martin wished he could argue, but he couldn't. It was his fault Mom was here. He had wanted to get her past the reach of the dreary suburb, but its reach was longer than he could have imagined.

"Why did we risk it?" Dad went on. "We can never make a life of it here, not without a fridge and a cooker and running water, not eating smoky fish three times a day. We should have stayed where there were people. People stick together, my dad always told me. But what did we do? We went off on our own."

Martin thought about how nice it would be if there were

people in this suburb. He would run next door for help, and the neighbors would come with little snacks and sit by Mom's bedside to cheer her up. And maybe he could play game cartridges with the kids who lived on his street.

But life here wasn't like that. Next door was nothing but a tangled mass of vines dragging down the ruined rafters, and instead of a cookie jar on the kitchen counter, there was a nest of little cranberry-colored birds. There weren't any people in this whole great outdoors who could be their friends. Except— Well, of course, Martin thought. Yes, of course!

He jumped up from the step and ran back into the house. "Where's my pack? I'm gonna go get help."

Mom sat on the bedroll, and Dad stood beside her while Martin split up the supplies.

"I don't think you should go," Mom said. "I'll be fine after a little rest, and I don't want you doing something dangerous."

Dad and Martin exchanged a look.

"It's just, you know, in case," Martin said. "Anyway, it's a short walk, probably just a day, and I'll have Chip with me to handle the danger."

Mom chewed her lower lip. "I don't like it. This is a lot of trouble over nothing."

"It'll give me a chance to check on Cassie and tell her about our new house," Martin said. "Remember, I've walked all over out here. It'll be fun. And maybe the prototypes can give us advice about how to fix this place up."

Dad asked, "So you think these prototype people will know about this?"

"They're really smart. They'll know what to do." Martin

hoped Theo would be home. It was over a week since he'd left. She was supposed to have reported back after five days.

"But why would they want to help?"

"They're nice." Most of them, at least, Martin thought. I'll just make sure William never goes near my dog.

Dad followed Martin into the kitchen to sort through the water bottles.

"But how do you know they have the resources?" he asked in a low voice. "You said Central is looking for them. What if they're in trouble of their own?"

"Nothing bad happens to them, Dad," Martin said. "They know just about everything."

Dad ran his hands through his thinning hair and rubbed them over his bald spot. He said, "I should be the one who goes."

No you shouldn't, Martin thought. You're old and out of shape, and you can't carry your own pack. Besides which, you don't even know the way. But he didn't say that. The secret of Dad's failings had become a burden he had to be man enough to carry.

"Look, you have to take care of Mom," he said as they took the bottles back to his other supplies. "You know how to fish and cook, and I don't."

At the mention of fishing, the troubled look on Dad's face eased. "I thought last night's catch turned out pretty well."

"It was lovely," Mom said, and he bent and kissed her. Martin felt better at the sight. After all, it was good that Mom and Dad didn't hate each other. It would be a lot worse if they did.

"Hey, Mom, I've got a present for you," he said. "Something you can paint pictures of."

He went to the kitchen and returned with the glass candy in its bowl. The sun coming through the windows lit fire in the hearts of the fanciful disks and sent a jewel-toned scattering of colored lights wavering over the walls and ceiling. Martin handed over his treasure with only a tiny twinge of regret. Probably, even though it was Mom's now, she'd still let him fool around with it sometimes.

"Martin!" Mom gasped. "Where did you find this?"

"It was the Owner's," he said. "But that's okay. It's yours now. Since you gotta sit here, at least you've got pretty things to look at." He picked up his knapsack and slung his water bottles over Chip. "I'll be back in a couple of days."

Dad followed them out of the house and stood on the steps to watch them leave. "Be careful!" he called.

Martin and Chip hurried up the road. Houses grew sparse, and the divided roadway dwindled to chunks of cracked and pitted asphalt. Where it crossed a dry streambed, segments of it had fallen in like folding leaves on a table, and green clumps of field grasses grew out of what remained. Then it made a long bend and began to rise. Martin put his head down and started to pant as the grade steepened. Chip quit bounding ahead.

After fifteen minutes, Martin paused to rest. He hadn't realized they'd climbed so high. Mom and Dad's new suburb was just a patch of forest behind him now, with a few dark squares of old houses poking through the leaves. Several miles farther off, back the way they had come, the steel dome of BNBRX created a white shimmer in the distance.

"We'll have to leave the road," he said. "We need to go straight this way, to the edge of those hills. That's where we'll find the dumps. I think I can just barely see them. And I think that might be the sawed-off cliff that's in front of the packet yard. If it is, we don't have too far to go."

After an afternoon of steady hiking, they reached the vast yard in the early evening. Packet cars of all descriptions sat silent on the wide fan of steel tracks. At the back, below the face of the steep cliff, the row of cinder-block sheds squatted in the sunshine. Chip wandered back and forth across the dusty ground and engaged in an orgy of sniffing.

"Hey, Theo left the shed with the tunnel unlocked," Martin said. "I know we locked it when we left."

They came through the long, boring tunnel and crossed the narrow valley dotted with fir trees. No children were playing outside. Martin located the shallow cave that led into the maze of classrooms. Its steel door was propped open with a metal wastebasket, and trash blew out under the trees.

"That's weird," Martin said.

School papers littered the corridor and rustled in small drifts against the wall. A plastic chair lay upended in a doorway. Water dripped in a hollow cadence somewhere nearby. It only served to accentuate the silence.

Chip sniffed the air and whined.

Martin walked down the hall, pushing open doors: empty classrooms, their desks tossed every which way; empty offices, their handhelds smashed, their stacks of papers flung down and stepped on. "No," Martin whispered. Then he ran. Up the stairs, to where Cassie lived. Where all the little children lived.

The dorm rooms were a chaotic jumble of broken bed frames and splintered nightstands. Mattresses straddled the wreckage, their pale stuffing spilling through long gashes. Drawers lay where they had been dumped out, and closet doors tilted from their runners. Chip pawed through the heaps of clothing and found a small brown object. He sniffed it all over, whimpering, and then dropped it at Martin's feet.

It was Cassie's stuffed bunny.

Martin stood rooted to the spot. Why hadn't he noticed the mud tracks in the tunnel, the crushed weeds outside? How could he be so blind? Strolling in here, expecting people to be ready to save the day—what a moron he'd turned out to be.

"This isn't happening!" he shouted. "Do you hear me? It's not *happening!*"

A distant voice sobbed out an answer. "Martin? Is that you?"

"Sim! Where are you? Where are you?"

Martin snatched up a baseball bat, staggered through the mounds of clothes, and threw himself down the stairs three steps at a time. Chip galloped beside him.

They found Sim lying hunched over against the wall of the cafeteria, his gray robes blending into the gray of the vinyl floor. A strange sound rose from his shaking lips, like the mewing of a cat.

"Martin!" cried the old bot, and he jerked up his face to look at them. Tears flowed down his wrinkled cheeks, but his eyes didn't look quite human. Their black pupils spun and flickered from diamond to point to round. Martin drew back and gripped the baseball bat tighter.

"Sim, are you okay?" he asked. "What happened? Where is everybody?"

"I don't remember," Sim sobbed. "Martin, I don't feel good." He'd begun to perspire, and his skin was pasty. "Something's happening to me. I can't stand up. I don't feel good."

"It's all right," Martin said. "You'll be okay." But all the same, he took a step back.

"Talking to you . . . it's done something," Sim gasped. He was sweating bullets now. "Martin!" he wailed. "I don't feel good!"

Big silver jelly drops rolled down Sim's face and slithered across his gray robes. Big silver jelly slugs wriggled from folds in his clothing and crawled onto the floor. One almost touched Martin's foot.

"Yeagh!" Martin screamed, and he brought down the baseball bat to smash it.

The slug exploded into a tassel of waving wires with a noise like an enraged Slinky. Quicker than Martin could think, the wires jerked their way up the baseball bat, pulling the tassel toward him like a spider. Other slugs nearby erupted into flailing bundles of wires, hissing and coiling.

Martin gave a yell, dropped the bat, and jumped onto the nearest table. The floor seethed with squirming silver things now, and the bat disappeared beneath wires.

"Martin!"

Pale eyes still stared out from the ruin of Sim's melting face. An odd gap of a mouth worked itself open, and sound blared out again.

"Martin! Get away! *Run!*"

CHAPTER ELEVEN

But Martin couldn't run. The slugs covered the floor nearby and trapped him on the cafeteria table. He turned around to locate an exit, and the slippery table rolled sideways, nearly flinging him off. A dozen slugs exploded with angry hisses, propelling their tasseled forms up the table's wheels and legs.

Fifteen feet away, Chip danced and barked at the edge of the widening tide. He ran up and down in front of the slugs' advance, trying to find a way back to his master.

"Hold on, Chip! Stay there. I'll come to you."

Martin tossed his knapsack onto a nearby table. It hit the center, slid along its sterile white length, and dropped off the opposite end. From its unseen location came a dozen pops and the furious sound of entangling wires. "Oh, crap!" he muttered. "That was a stupid move."

The wire monsters had surmounted the legs and benches of the table Martin was on. Silver wires were grappling the edges of the tabletop. He jumped and landed heavily on a nearby table. It rolled forward through a buzz of springing wires. How many slug traps could Sim melt into? Several hundred? A thousand?

The slug army continued to advance, wriggling outward in a wide circle. If the squirmy things got to the door before he did, his escape would be cut off. Martin flung himself onto another table and skinned his elbow. He almost slipped over the edge. Then he lay there for a few seconds, listening to his heartbeat and peeking at the writhing uproar below him.

Chip's barks changed into howls.

The German shepherd danced at the edge of the fray, still beyond the reach of the slugs, but in his anxiety over Martin, he had forgotten his own safety. He had let the spreading tide trap him on the side of the cafeteria that didn't have a door.

"Get onto a table!" Martin yelled.

But Chip wasn't near a table. The nearest row of tables was at least twelve feet away. If Chip had been thinking like a bot, he could have walked straight up the wall. But, panicked and threatened, separated from his master, Chip's thinking was all dog. He crouched down, collected himself, and sprang.

He almost made it.

Chip's forepaws landed on the tabletop. His back paws landed on the bench. One paw slipped off and touched the ground. Martin saw a flash of something silver. With a shriek, Chip bounded into the air and rolled off the table. He almost disappeared beneath a volley of silver wires.

"Chip! No!" Martin screamed.

Chip flailed and kicked under the coating of wires. Martin saw them vanish tassel by tassel, as if they had burrowed beneath the dog's skin. Chip's terrified cries abruptly changed into a mechanical screech. His writhing form froze into bizarre poses, as if he were caught in the beam of a strobe light.

"Chip, hold on! I'm coming!"

Martin threw himself blindly from table to table, heedless of the pop and flash of seething wires. The bow wave of gray slugs reached the door and cut off his escape, but he didn't care anymore. He wasn't escaping. He was going to save his dog. At the moment, nothing else mattered.

He jumped, misjudged the distance, and slipped. A second later, he found himself sitting on the table's bench with one leg dangling to the floor. Before he could curl it back, it touched a slug.

Pop!

A small silver buzz saw appeared to erupt from the slug and took aim at his sneaker with a metallic zing. Many short wires whirled through the air and hooked themselves onto his foot. Flinging themselves in arcs, the wires jerked their way up the laces, pulled onto his sock, and grappled for purchase on his pant leg. Then two long wires met around his ankle, and the entire flailing mass followed their lead. Before Martin could blink, they had smoothed into a silver band, as snug as half a set of handcuffs. He sat and stared dumbly at it while the army of slugs passed by him and seized upon the rocking wheels of his table.

As the uproar died down, he heard a desolate whimper. Chip!

"I'm coming," he said, and climbed to his feet. An electrical jolt flashed through him and left him giddy.

Chip's whining grew desperate.

"Give me just a minute," he said as he took another step. This time the world went away. It came back a little later, but it came back as ceiling tiles. Martin discovered that he was lying on his back.

Over the ringing in his ears, he heard a mechanical alarm-clock screech. Cautiously, he turned his head. Chip was blinking in and out—dog, blur, dog, blur—with the dark rect-angles of two circuit boards showing through his hazy form like shadows on an X-ray.

Martin's teeth hurt, and his whole body felt tired, as if he'd been flinging giant boulders around. A straggler slug slipped past his shoulder, and he shuddered involuntarily. It burst like a cascaron and jerked itself into a band around his arm.

"Don't move, Chip," he muttered. "They zap you if you move. They won't let us go anywhere. Just do what I do. Take a little nap. Close your eyes for a while."

When he opened his eyes again, the room was silent, and he was stiff from lying so long. The slug army was gone. He stared at the ceiling tiles for a few minutes. How long have I been here? he thought. He was afraid to lift his hand to check his watch.

Chip was a normal dog again. He lay on his haunches a few feet away, dolefully licking a foot. When he saw Martin glance toward him, he dropped his big head onto his forepaws and gave a breathy little whine.

"Hey, buddy," Martin whispered back. "I'm right here. We're gonna do this together." He closed his eyes again.

After eons, they heard firm footsteps in the hall, and Chip's ears swiveled forward. "Shh," Martin said before the dog could bark. He turned his head toward the doorway, laying his cheek against the cool floor. A saltines packet and the end of a bitten carrot stick lay a couple of feet away.

The steps grew louder, and someone came into the room. Tabletops blocked Martin's view of all but the person's olive-gray lace-up boots. Then the boots came around the end of the nearest table, and their owner came into view.

It was a military police bot. Martin had seen them in governmental parades on the nightly news. Battalions of these gray-faced bots marched by the cameras in their uniforms of dusty green. Martin remembered the Great Battery Panic that had occurred when he was five, when faulty rechargeables had shut down the cookers and custodial bots and trash had piled up for weeks. The news had shown packet cars full of military police bots deployed to the worst-hit suburbs, hand-delivering sacks of trash to the loading bays, vacuuming school rooms, and restoring order. Martin hadn't forgiven Dad for organizing citizen's brigades to haul off their own garbage because it kept the military police from coming to help.

He'd always thought the reason the bots appeared to have no expressions under their green helmets was because that the cameras were too far away to catch them. Now he learned the true reason: the bots had no faces. This soldier had nothing but a sketchy suggestion of features on its iron gray head. It had a prominent chin and straight nose, but no mouth to speak of; a serious slant to its brows, but no eyes. Its gray hands grasped a heavy assault rifle.

"Your name and place of origin," it barked.

Martin was afraid to sit up. If the slugs shocked him and he went into a fit, the soldier might decide to shoot him. He lay on his back and held out his hands in what he hoped was a nonthreatening gesture. "I don't know what 'origin' is," he said.

Chip vibrated out a message in bot-to-bot protocol. A change came over the soldier at once.

"Sir!" the soldier said. Dark blue dye swept across its green uniform like a cloud blotting out the sun. Bright ribbons sprouted across its chest in a colorful row, gold braid rolled down its trouser legs, and its helmet engaged in some serious origami. Within seconds, the soldier stood at attention in a dark blue service cap and full dress uniform, a drill rifle with a rubbed walnut stock by its side.

"It is an *honor*, sir!" the soldier said. "I apologize for your detention. We had no warning Central was sending a delegation to this site. I'll have you out of those traps in no time."

Martin glanced from the soldier to his dog. Chip's tail whapped against the floor. Martin felt a movement at his shoulder, and the bundle of wires there fell to the floor with a plop. In another second, the wires at his ankle did the same. Chip stood up and shook, and silver tassels flew in all directions. They skidded along benches and landed in limp little piles.

"Please allow me to assist you to your feet, sir," the soldier said. He extended a gray hand.

"Um . . . sure, thanks," Martin said. The hand didn't feel like he thought it would. It was cool and smooth, like a plastic milk jug.

"Lieutenant, you found one!"

A man in a gray suit stepped into the cafeteria. A second gray-suited man followed him. "No, he's not a Wonder Baby," the second man said. "He's too old."

"It's the A and Z guys!" Martin cried. There was no mistaking the watery eyes, snub noses, and fish-mouth frowns.

"How does he know our names, Zeb?" the first agent asked uneasily.

Agent Zebulon ignored him.

"Your name and place of origin," he snapped to Martin. "And— Great glory! Lieutenant, why are you in dress blues?"

The soldier bot's posture was stiff with reproach. "Agent, you failed to notify my task force that we would be encountering privileged personnel. This boy represents a delegation from Central."

The two agents turned their frowns on Martin. They looked like playground bullies, fighters who would do anything to win, even if they had to cheat. "Central's sending out kids now?" Zebulon said. "We'll just see about that."

Before Martin could react, the agents seized his arms, and the two of them frog-marched him over to a table. They twisted him around so that the bench caught him behind the knees, and he sat down hard. A bright light flashed in his eyes, and he cupped his hands over them, blinking.

"Take a look at that," Zebulon murmured, holding a small handheld out to Abel.

"'Martin Revere Glass,'" Abel read from its screen. "The . . . the one with the bot! The bot in the plot!"

"That's enough, Abel. You sound like an idiot."

"The plot against the Secretary of—"

"Shut *up*!"

"Let go of me!" Martin yelled, thrashing. "Chip, over here! Help!"

But for the first time, Chip didn't come to his aid. The German shepherd didn't seem to know what to do. He barked ferociously and snapped at the agents, but his teeth didn't make contact. When one of the agents turned and tried to grab him, he yelped and slipped out of reach.

"Stop squirming, kid." Zebulon delivered a quick blow to Martin's chest, and Martin gasped for breath. "And you, bot, stop that barking!" Chip's howls turned to breathy whines.

Meanwhile, the soldier had been keeping up a steady stream of indignant protests. "In accordance with Battlefield Directive 182-dash-34, Central personnel are never to be—"

Abel interrupted him. "Soldier, this boy is a fugitive. He tricked you. You're malfunctioning. Shut down and perform diagnostics."

"Negative, sir! I was informed of his clearance by the canine officer."

Abel and Zebulon turned to Chip again. The dog crouched on his belly now, watching them with pricked ears.

"A canine *officer*," Abel said.

"Like a canine *colleague*," Zebulon murmured. "Or a *partner*." His eyes took on an ominous gleam. "Good work apprehending these two, Lieutenant. We'll take it from here. Abel, not another word from anybody till we get these two in the packet."

The soldier blocked their way.

"Do I have to remind you, sir," the soldier said icily, "that you need a directive signed by the Special Prosecution Team to arrest a Central government official? I've radioed Central about the irregularity of this event. No one moves till we get an answer."

Abel rolled his eyes. "Oh, for the love of—" Zebulon stopped him.

"Lieutenant, you—you what?" Zebulon said. "You say you've radioed Central?"

"And they've radioed back," the soldier announced with satisfaction. "Switching to send/receive video mode."

The gray-faced bot's brass buttons and row of bright parade ribbons dissolved into shiny blackness. In the middle of his chest, a dark square appeared. It flickered, and Martin realized with a jolt that it was a television.

A man's face peered out from the television screen, a large, florid face like a honey-baked ham. Fleshy eyelids pouched protectively around the man's brown eyes, almost closing them, and two small, neat ears tilted away from the massive forehead like the cropped ears of a Great Dane. The man's head met his body without the intervention of a neck: a black suit coat sloped out almost immediately below the little ears, and the Windsor knot of a red silk necktie sheltered beneath his formidable chin. A white headline banner at the bottom of the screen carried his title: SECRETARY OF STATE.

"What's going on here?" the Secretary demanded.

"Oh, crap!" muttered Zebulon.

CHAPTER TWELVE

"What's this about?" the Secretary of State said again. "Agents. Still got your hair. Young agents. X, Y, or Z batch, I'd say."

"Sir, I'm Agent Zebulon," Zebulon declared, stepping in front of Martin. "My junior partner here is Agent Abel."

Martin peeked around Zebulon's pinstripe back in time to see the Secretary's tiny eyes narrow shrewdly. "The A batch is productive already, eh?"

Zebulon coughed. "More or less."

"What's going on? An alert came through that a Central official was where he didn't belong. It's a good thing I wasn't asleep."

"Yes, sir."

"I *never* sleep, Agent Zebulon."

"Yes, sir. I'd heard that, sir. I'm very sorry you were disturbed. Actually, that report came to you in error. The military bot appears to have malfunctioned."

The soldier providing the video feed couldn't appear in his own defense, but he bristled and protested. "Negative, sir! My internal diagnostics indicate that I am one hundred percent mission ready. I can dump the codes to any handheld you wish."

"Thank you, thank you, soldier," the Secretary told him smoothly. "I'll get to the bottom of this."

"The lieutenant appears to believe," Zebulon said, "that a teenage boy is on the payroll at Central. But we'll take care of it, sir. We'll make sure his circuit board gets the maintenance it needs."

The Secretary of State's tone sharpened with interest. "Who's that?"

"Who's what, sir? The soldier? He's Lieutenant Bravo-Bravo-Romeo-Tango."

"Not him, Agent! The boy. Get out of my way." Zebulon moved aside with reluctance, and the face on the television screen drank Martin in. "A Wonder Baby. By Jove, you've got one!"

"No, sir, I'm afraid not. This is a regular older-model boy."

"Aren't you at the Wonder Baby school? Or did Lieutenant Tango get that wrong too?"

Zebulon answered, after just a hint of a hesitation, "No, sir, he was right about that."

The Secretary of State looked baffled. "Where the devil did that boy come from, then?"

"Well, we went to retrieve him from his suburb, sir . . ."

"Negative!" barked the soldier. "I apprehended him right here in this room."

Impatience clouded the Secretary's expression, and a dent formed in the middle of his forehead. "Agent, answer me! Did you bring that boy here or not?"

"We intended to, sir. But there was—ah—interference. We intended to interrogate him just now, but that's when the soldier malfunctioned."

"Intended. Intended! I don't care what you intended. Don't you even know his name?"

Zebulon paused and smoothed his pinstripe sleeves,

doubtless looking for inspiration on his cuffs. Abel shifted from foot to foot and then blurted into the silence, "Sir, the soldier shouldn't have bothered you. This kid is nobody important. Nothing for you to worry about."

The Secretary's broad face turned red. "Ah! Thank you, young sprat, for your kind thoughts on my behalf. So I don't need to worry?"

"No, sir."

"Would you like to know how I got to be three times your age? By worrying when I didn't need to worry. Would you like to know how many assassination plots I've survived? Twenty-seven. One of them involved poisoned socks."

"Um . . . yes, sir."

"And would you like to know how many agents I've had to execute for involvement in those plots? Thirty-eight agents, Agent. Two agents from the L batch, eight agents from the O batch, six agents from the Q batch (the names those men had!), four agents from the S batch, ten agents from the V batch, one W, six Xs, and one Y. Did you by any chance know the man from the Y batch, Agent?"

Abel gulped. "Yorick. Yes, sir. I remember him."

"Go on remembering him," the Secretary advised. "It'll keep you out of trouble. And now, both of you, get out of the way."

The agents moved back. Martin jumped. The Secretary was staring right at him. His gaze made Principal Thomasson's stare seem soppily sentimental.

"Young man! Do you by any chance have a name?"

"Yes . . . um . . . sir."

Martin paused. The Secretary's eyes skewered him. Chip

cowered a few feet away, belly to the floor. The two agents watched him contemptuously out of the corners of their eyes: *It's not us on the hot seat anymore.*

"My name, sir." He licked his lips. "It's Martin, sir. Martin . . . um . . . Glass."

The fat eyelids opened wide. "You're the boy who escaped from a collector!"

Martin licked his lips again. "Yes, sir. I guess you could say that."

The Secretary's stare turned elsewhere.

"Agent Zebulon, Agent Abel, you are relieved of your interrogation duties. I'm coming to take care of this in person. Lieutenant, stand watch over this young man and detain him safely. Don't let anyone but me or my personal security detail come within five feet of him. You have your orders. I'm on my way."

The television on the soldier's chest flickered out. Like stars, the brass buttons returned one by one to their royal blue field.

Agent Zebulon continued to stand, deadpan, for a slow count of ten. Then his fist shot out and clipped Abel's ear.

"You *idiot*!" he yelled. "You freaking disgrace to your DNA! I can't believe I have to share your genes, you stupid pissant."

Abel clutched his ear. "Ow!"

The soldier bot stiff-armed both agents out of the way. "Please step back from my detainee. If you wouldn't mind taking a seat, sir," he said to Martin. "We have a long wait before us."

Abel and Zebulon sank down onto a nearby bench and brooded, their empty hands open on their gray pinstripe knees. "The Secretary doesn't know about the bot," Abel murmured. "What do you say we—"

"Chip, get over here," Martin called sharply.

"Abel, shut your mouth! Seriously, do you have a death wish?"

Chip scuttled to Martin's side and put his head on Martin's knee. The agents watched him with identical disgusted looks and fell to brooding again.

Abel stirred. "Well, we could—"

"Shut up."

"I know, but we could just—"

"Shut *up*!"

Martin noted the exchange with grim satisfaction.

"So, your walls have ears too, huh?" he said. "Even you guys. What about eyeballs? Do your walls have those?"

Abel cracked his knuckles. "Don't get smart. We're the eyeballs on your walls, kid."

"Well, not now, you're not," Martin said. "What did you losers do with my little sister?"

Zebulon propped his elbows on his knees and sank his chin onto his folded hands. "Where are your parents, kid?" he countered. "We're only asking because we care."

That shot hit home. Martin's throat tightened at the thought of Mom. "Leave me alone," he muttered.

"Hey, look, Abel, trouble," Zebulon said, nudging his partner's foot with his. "What is it, bad food? Broken leg? Poison ivy? I bet we could help Mom and Dad, couldn't we?"

"We'd love to," Abel said solemnly. "We live to serve."

"You don't serve my parents," Martin snapped. "You were gonna arrest them in the middle of the night!"

Zebulon's expression didn't change, but Abel drew back,

bewildered. "How did he know that? Is it because of his— Ow!" Zebulon had snapped his finger against Abel's temple.

"You came here to get help," Zebulon decided after a pause. "Mom, or Dad? Mom?"

Martin hunched his shoulders. "Don't talk about my mom."

"Mom, then. What happened? You can tell us."

"You losers know what happened! You shut up about my mom!"

"We know, huh? Interesting." Zebulon studied Martin keenly. "Mom's in trouble, and we're supposed to know about it. Now, see, Abel, that's what we call a clue."

Martin bit his lip. "Just shut up," he whispered.

"Oh, you think we're not playing nice?" Zebulon said. "Just wait till the Secretary of State gets here. You think it's some kind of prize to get the most powerful man in the nation out of bed? Think again."

"Yeah, squirt," Abel said. "Zebulon and I just arrest people. The Secretary of State makes an example out of them."

Martin bent his head and petted Chip. I'm not scared, he told himself. I've faced down a collector before. But he remembered how scary that had been, and he knew he was kidding himself.

"But that's not as bad as the interrogation," Zebulon pointed out. "The Secretary of State has the twelve Ursulas."

"That's right." Abel's voice was low. "The Ursulas. They look like women."

"Like big tall women," Zebulon said. "Like big tall *scary* women. But they're not."

Martin thought about Dad in his best suit, waiting to face

Truth in the Mayor's packet car. Dad's eyes had been black with terror.

"The twelve Ursulas. Every one of them knows how to kill. In fact, that's about all they know how to do. The Secretary of State once had them kill a gorilla on a bet. You know what a gorilla is, right?"

"A hairy monster," Martin muttered. "House-to-House Number Five."

"The Ursulas killed him with their bare hands."

"*Bare hands*," Abel echoed, nodding. "They say the Ursulas can rip the heart out of your chest and hold it up in front of you, and you can watch it *beat* before you die."

Martin pushed Chip's head from his lap and jumped to his feet.

"Okay, seriously, are you guys part of a comedy show, or what?" he said. "Because you guys would be a riot on television."

The soldier bot laid a gentle hand on his shoulder. "Sir, please don't get excited."

Zebulon grinned. "If you don't believe us," he said, "ask Bravo-Bravo-Romeo here. Bravo, Romeo! Bravo! Come on, Abel, you moron, we might as well go write our report."

The two agents strolled out of the room. "That's Bravo-Bravo-Romeo-*Tango*," the soldier called after them.

Lieutenant Tango brought Martin a blanket from his knapsack. "I believe you'll need this to rest properly," he said. "Do you need anything else?"

"I'm kinda hungry," Martin muttered. "Do they have cookers here? Or could you bring me something from the cafeteria fridge?"

"The refrigerators are empty, and I'm afraid the cookers are nonstandard."

"Oh . . . well, some water, then," Martin suggested.

"The faucets aren't operating."

In the end, the soldier brought Martin his mostly empty water bottle and a squashed energy bar.

Martin lay on his blanket on the floor tiles, blinking at the big lights overhead. His spirits were so low that he could barely think straight. He didn't know what to do. The thought of the smooth, sly Secretary headed his way made the pit of his stomach hurt, and the idea of Mom and Dad waiting for him to bring help made him miserable. As for the school, he couldn't even think about it. Cassie was only six years old. And now . . .

Cassie's supposed to be here, he thought. I left her right here in this room. The prototypes were supposed to take care of her. I trusted them, and they let me down. But Cassie trusted me. And I let something bad happen to my little sister.

He fell into a fitful sleep, and he dreamt.

He and Cassie were at the park together, and he was following her up the tall ladder at the slide to make sure she didn't fall. He was scolding her about it, telling her she was a baby for making him do it, but she was smiling anyway. All that mattered was that her big brother was there for her. It didn't matter how much he complained.

And then she was slipping down the big yellow slide, her little hands poised over the high slide rails to slow herself down if she went too fast. She was laughing out loud, and her tight golden ringlets bobbed around her head. She landed on her feet in a spray of gravel and yelled for him to follow her. "Come on, come on!" she called, bouncing up and down in her white sneakers. "I want to go again."

We aren't really at the park, he thought. Cassie's not really here. He knew it because of the misery that filled him.

"Martin's scared," she sang. "Scared of the slide. Come on!" Her eyes were blue, the turquoise blue of a clear sunny sky, a little piece of sky inside the suburb.

This is just a memory, Martin thought, from a couple of months ago, when she lost her first tooth. I'm about to go down the slide, and she's too close to it, and my foot kicks her, and her loose tooth flies out. And I think she's gonna cry and run home and tell Mom, but she's so happy about the tooth that she doesn't.

As he thought these things, they happened just the way he remembered them. He loosed his hands, and he flew down the long fiberglass slide. He saw the uncertainty in Cassie's big blue eyes just before his foot connected with her. He saw her spin around and hit the gravel, and he braced himself for the tears. But her gap-toothed smile was radiant as she got to her knees and held the pearly little tooth in the air.

"I've got one for the tooth fairy! I've got one!"

Martin sat straight up on his bedroll and opened his eyes. "Chip!" he cried. "Wake up! They haven't got them!"

Chip scrambled to his feet while Martin hugged his knees to his chest and thought about what he had heard. *You got one,* the Secretary had said when he thought Martin was a Wonder Baby. But nobody would say that about the thousandth kid they caught, or be as excited as the Secretary had looked, either.

You got one, meaning the first one, just like Cassie's tooth. The Wonder Babies had gotten away.

The joy Martin felt left him breathless. Cassie was safe. The gas masks and evacuation drills had worked.

Ears pricked, Chip was nosing him in the face, trying to figure out what he was talking about. But the walls had ears, and so did the military bot. Martin jumped to his feet.

"What are you doing?" Lieutenant Tango asked. "You can't leave. I have to detain you."

Martin stopped to think. What were the Secretary's exact words? Exact words mattered to a bot.

Don't let anyone but me or my personal security detail come within five feet of him.

"You're too close to me," Martin said. "The Secretary says only his security guys can get this close. Move back."

Lieutenant Tango shook his head, but he took a step back. "You still have to stay here."

"Or you'll—what? Shoot me?" Martin said. He started walking backward away from the soldier, holding his hands out wide. "You can't shoot me, the Secretary said I have to be safe. Hey, stay back, five feet away."

The bot's blank face managed to convey helpless confusion. "But I have to detain you!"

"Tell you what," Martin suggested, reaching out to guide himself through the doorway, "detain me while I walk."

Lieutenant Tango halted abruptly. Chip skidded to a stop and barked. Martin turned around and looked up. A long way up.

A broad face was looking down at him. "You need to come with us," it said.

CHAPTER THIRTEEN

Twelve women walked into the cafeteria and fanned out in a half circle around Martin. They were copies of one another; or rather, they were one woman, multiplied twelve times. They—or she—stood seven feet tall and were bulky to match, so that Martin felt like a preschooler beside them. They—the shes—wore navy blue military jumpsuits, a style of clothing that seemed like somebody's idea of a cruel joke, emphasizing just how out of shape they were. Their figures were the sort euphemistically described as pear-shaped, with a cellulite jiggle around the thighs.

The faces of the twelve women—one face multiplied twelve times—were the kind Martin saw with his mom at school meetings and immediately forgot. Their hair was cut into a particularly unfashionable pageboy, mostly blond with half an inch of brown roots. Their eyes were small and patient and half-buried in wrinkles, and their cheeks drooped into their jaws and pulled their cupid's-bow mouths into sad little lines. Martin wasn't sure they could smile even if they wanted to.

"The Ursulas!" Martin whispered.

Chip addressed them in bot, and then they addressed one another. They didn't vibrate—at least, not as far as Martin could tell—but they conveyed by tiny gestures and glances the idea of a conversation rapidly transmitted.

"You need to come with us, Martin Glass," the first one said again, towering over him.

"Okay," he said, conscious of how high his voice sounded after hers. "I just—well, I just gotta check this one thing."

He turned to Lieutenant Tango. Next to the Ursulas, the soldier seemed silly and artificial, like an inflated action figure. "Is it true what the agents said about them?" Martin whispered. "About ripping people apart with their bare hands?"

The lead Ursula spoke up. "We generally dislocate or fracture the cervical vertebrae. Body fluids stain carpets and wall coverings." Her expression was as bland and long-suffering as if she were complaining that she couldn't get her shirt collars white.

"Oh!" Martin's voice was very high now. It seemed to have gone up an octave. "Oh, wow. That's all I needed to know. Thanks, ma'am."

"Are you ready to go?"

"You bet," Martin said. So she hoisted his knapsack and held out her hand, and he took it as if he were three.

They walked down the hall, past broken handhelds and sheets of paper that swirled by the open doors. Outside was the gray hush that comes just before dawn. White tendrils of cloud seemed to have drifted down from the sky and woven a net among the trunks of the dripping fir trees. The Ursulas walked into the net of cloud, and Martin found that it was chilly.

The cold air helped to focus his thoughts and free him from the feeling of awe that the Ursulas had inspired. The important thing, he reminded himself, was that the prototypes had done it. They had moved the school. That means Cassie's safe, he thought, and that means the plan is still on. I have to find them and get them to help Mom.

But that meant getting away from the Secretary of State. Even the agents were afraid of him.

"What's this Secretary guy like?" he asked the Ursula who held his hand. "Is he nice?"

"No."

"Why do you work for him, then?"

"We don't," Ursula answered. "Our duty is to protect and defend the President. But the President told us to protect and defend the Secretary of State."

"So who's defending the President while you're gone?"

Ursula pondered. "I don't know."

They were climbing out of the valley, clambering from boulder to boulder to get to the entrance of the tunnel. Martin wasn't sorry to have a strong hand to hold. He knew the Ursulas were killers, but their morose pessimism wasn't nearly as frightening as the obsessive enthusiasm of collector bots.

Besides, Cassie was free. That was half his worry gone. But where was she? How had they gotten away? The red packet car. Martin was sure of it. The Wonder Babies were too little to make an escape on foot.

He was walking through the long tunnel now. The Ursulas filled it up completely. They had to stoop in order not to bump their heads. Martin felt a little claustrophobic at the center of their crowd. All he could see were generous blue backs and upholstered blue fronts, like an escort of massive pillows. As the Ursulas swung their flashlights, strange shadows formed and jumped from place to place.

The prototypes must have used the red packet car; it was longer than a regular packet, so it could hold lots of kids, and it had controls a human could work. But it was also conspicuous. That meant no traveling near cameras. There was a camera near BNBRX, so they wouldn't have gone that way. Where else was there a camera? Martin didn't know, but at least he had a place to start looking.

He came out of the tunnel to a band of sky on the horizon that had lightened to the color of dust. "Hey, I left something over this way," he told the Ursulas. "Do you mind if we walk by to get it?"

"Will it help the interrogation?" Ursula asked.

"Maybe," Martin lied.

Sure enough, the red packet car was gone. Nothing was left but a wasp's nest hanging from the rafter under the tin roof and a faint shine on the empty rails.

"Sorry," Martin said. "It's not here. No help."

The Ursulas looked deeply disappointed. But then, they always did.

They led him past the rusted, peeling packet cars to the front of the rail yard, where the single set of tracks branched out into three pairs of rails, then five, then more. At the head of this steel delta stood a short packet car, shadowy and anonymous in the poor light. Ursula helped Martin up onto the open grillwork of its small platform.

The interior was cozy, with dark walnut paneling and polished brass fixtures. A boy, a dog, and twelve large Ursulas made it cozier still. Martin took his seat as directed on a tapestry-covered bench that jutted out from the wall.

Next to the bench, a large picture window with crystal-clear glass framed the shifting colors of dawn. When Martin leaned close, it played mirror as well and showed him his own dim reflection. I'm about to meet a good friend of the President, he thought, and it's been two days since I brushed my teeth.

Across from Martin, sharing his picture window, squatted a generously proportioned leather armchair. An Ursula unfolded a stowaway end table beside it while another Ursula knocked on a door in the front wall.

"Good morning," she called.

Thumps and bumps erupted in the room beyond. Then came the sound of running water. Chip wormed his way through the crowd of Ursulas to lean up against Martin's bench. He was panting a little from the close quarters and the excitement.

"Hey, buddy," Martin whispered to him. "We need to find a way out of here. Mom's counting on us to get help."

The knob turned, and a hairy arm with rolled-up sleeves pushed the door open. The Secretary of State stumbled out. His face was as red as a beefsteak and shiny with sweat. He had abandoned his coat and tie, and his shirt had pulled out from his creased trousers. He tucked it back in as he staggered through the door.

The Secretary collapsed into the armchair, which gave a loud, protesting creak, and he glared at them all through sleep-filmed eyes. The Ursulas gathered around and ministered to him as if he were critically ill.

"Here's your coffee."

A steaming mug the size of a soup bowl appeared on the stowaway table. The Secretary fumbled for the handle without looking, and Ursula turned the cup so it would meet his groping hand.

"Ugh," he muttered, or something that sounded like it, and hid his face behind the wide brim. It parted from the mug shinier than ever.

An Ursula laid a white porcelain saucer on the table and dropped two large brown pills onto it with a sharp, high-pitched tinkle. The Secretary winced and swore at her, swept the pills up in a large fist, and consumed them with the next swig of coffee.

Martin brightened a little. Maybe we'll get breakfast, he thought. I'm pretty hungry—okay, really hungry. Really thirsty, too.

An Ursula pressed a panel, and it slid aside to reveal a television screen. The President was silently talking. She touched a button, and his voice filled the crowded packet car, the same earnest voice Martin had grown up hearing every morning.

"You have voted to authorize Poison Safety Day," the President was saying. "A day to examine your cabinets and check the expiration dates on your medications to be sure your family is safe from accidental injury."

The Secretary of State leaned toward the television screen, his coffee cup halfway to his face. His incoherent grumbling smoothed out into a purr.

"My dear fellow citizens," continued the President, "my dear men, women, and children of this great and prosperous land, if Poison Safety Day saves only one life, it will be—" The Secretary gestured, and the television went black.

Confused, Martin looked at the saffron-tinted sky. Then he checked his watch. "Hey, wait a minute," he said. "It's not seven o'clock yet. Nobody's done their voting."

The Secretary took a noisy swallow of coffee. "Oh, Lord," he mumbled. "An idealist!" Another Ursula counted out several tan capsules of various sizes, and he swept them into his mouth with a martyred expression.

Martin still gazed at the black television screen, trying to sort out what that meant. "He looks so sad," he remarked, remembering what Mom had said. "He looks tired all the time these days."

That was how he learned that the Secretary had a very unpleasant laugh.

Several more brown bottles of pills came and went, along with the sound of slurping and crunching. Martin climbed onto his knees on the bench to watch the sunrise.

The sky in the east warmed by the second until it was a delicate magenta haze. Then the sun progressed in unhurried fashion over the horizon. It widened from a rim of orange to a great ruby circle that shimmered like an organdy party dress.

"Wow," Martin breathed, unable to tear his eyes away. "You gotta get a look at that!"

The Secretary of State put down his empty coffee mug. He muttered, "You can't make a dime off a sunrise."

An Ursula took the cup away while another put away all the pills. Several more Ursulas stood by the controls. The packet car lurched and started to roll.

"But people would like to see it," Martin pointed out. "Everything doesn't have to cost money."

"You talk like a subversive," the Secretary said. "So, you think things ought to be free."

Philosophy wasn't Martin's strong suit, and neither was

politics, but he did feel strongly about sunrises. "Well, it shouldn't be a crime to come out and look around," he said. "People could go back inside, and it would be fine."

"That shows what you know," the Secretary said scornfully. "Ursula! Slower! You're upsetting my stomach." The car slowed down, and he rested his massive forehead on his hand. "What do you know?" he grumbled with his eyes closed. "You don't even know what suburbs are for."

"We're the lucky ones," Martin recited. "Our grandparents competed for the right to live in comfort—"

"Blah, blah, blah." The Secretary leaned back in his armchair and stuck a hand inside his shirtfront to scratch. "Ursula, how long till I get out of this pigsty?"

"At this speed, seventeen hours."

"Oh, hell! Speed up, then. Just mind the bumps, will you?" He dropped his head onto his hands again.

Martin watched the landfills slide by. First the shoe dump. Then the plastic dump. How far away could the Wonder Babies be?

"Those lucky suburbs," continued the Secretary with his hand over his eyes, "are nothing more than focus groups. Market test audiences." He enunciated the words carefully, as if he could taste them in his mouth. "We give the suburbs a little money, and they indicate which products they like. They show us what's out of date and which commercials work. Our corporations produce these products in large quantities, which they sell in similar ad campaigns overseas. There, less enlightened countries, stuffed to the seams with surplus people, buy our products by the billions."

He fixed Martin with his disagreeable stare, made more disturbing by the light pink hue of his bloodshot eyes.

"For the privilege of being 'world leaders' and doing business from our shores, these corporations pay our government fantastic sums. Central laps up the cream and skims off a little whey to keep the suburbs happy, and the whole world spins along like a top. But you think we should give it all up to scratch in the dirt and watch the sun rise."

The Secretary brooded over Martin. Martin knew to keep his mouth shut now. Every teacher from kindergarten up had brooded over him. Principal Thomasson had practically made a career out of it.

"Martin Revere Glass, from Suburb HM1," he said. "You know something I don't. And that makes me very unhappy."

Martin kept his face blank. That was all a kid could do when adults were brooding.

"Even worse," the Secretary continued, "the agents are after you because they appear to know something I don't. And that makes me very concerned. Do you know how many members of our Central government have suffered assassination in recent years? Forty-four. And I only ordered half of them."

The Secretary cupped his chin in his hands and pulled absently at the folds of his neck.

"Martin Revere Glass," he said again, "who has done the impossible, who enters and leaves suburbs at will. Who defied a collector and spirited away a packet chief. I believe you have a story to tell me."

Martin felt his cheeks flush under the Secretary's relentless stare. He reached down to pet his dog and discovered that Chip had slunk out of sight around the edge of the bench. Chip has the right idea, he thought.

"Ursula!" called the Secretary. "Bring me my handheld. Mr. Glass—get to talking. Now."

So Martin talked. Some of it was the truth. Not much of it, but some.

"How did you get out of the suburb?" the Secretary growled at one point.

"Rolled," Martin said.

"On what?"

Martin waved his hands. "On a packet thing. The nets catch you if you walk."

They came to the junction, where the packet lines split four ways. Martin felt the packet rattle and sway from side to side as they rolled over the switch. But they didn't turn, and before long, bright green produce fields flowed by.

Like I don't have enough to worry about, Martin thought. Now we're heading for the old suburb. But maybe the Wonder Babies came this way too.

"Why did you leave the suburb?" the Secretary prompted as Martin fell silent. "Everything you wanted was there."

"I told you, my sister was gone."

"A Wonder Baby! Little parasites!" The Secretary's face darkened, and he heaved in his seat like bubbling oatmeal. "They're a menace to society! They belong in a cage in a lab."

Martin was too shocked to reply. He resumed his rambling story. As he talked, he scanned the scenery for clues.

"You say you found the tunnel to the hidden school by

accident," the Secretary interrupted a few minutes later. "I've seen pictures. It's not easy to find."

"I just got lucky, I guess."

Sooner than Martin would have believed possible, they reached the massive aerial knot of roads and passed beneath it into the haunted suburbs. The packet car slowed down. Battered houses covered in vines began drifting past. Martin wondered how many skeletons they held.

The Secretary broke into Martin's completely pointless digression about how to choose the perfect campsite. "Where are your parents now?"

"I dunno," Martin said. And he didn't, not for sure. He eyed the damaged houses. Skeleton houses, he thought. Each with its own skeleton family.

"So you just split up from your parents, went off on your own, left them in the wilderness without a backward glance. And you're telling me you did that—why?"

"A kid gets tired of hanging around with his mom and dad all the time." That was the truth, one hundred percent.

Ruined buildings gathered by the tracks in greater and greater numbers, big brick boxes several stories high. Rusted wire fences cordoned off the weedy spaces between them. Streets were everywhere now, some mere suggestions buried under generations of leaves, others with most of their concrete intact beneath a sprinkling of spindly weeds. Dark metal hulks on wheels sat in neat rows along them. Each hulk was large enough to hold an entire family at once, with a rusted roof overhead to keep off the rain. A tiny steel dome, Martin thought.

"Well, well," the Secretary said when Martin came to the end of his story. "That's quite an improbable tale."

"Thanks," Martin murmured.

The old city spread out around them, full of useless junk of all sizes, from the derelict buildings sporting caved-in doors to the cascades of ancient trash that spilled out of every storefront and choked the busted sidewalks. Discolored signs still lined the streets. Those that he could make out made no sense. QUICK WASH. U-FIX. DRY CLEAN. HANDI LUBE. What a weird world.

I bet the Wonder Babies came this way, he thought. There's lots of cover, lots of room to hide. That's important. You can't stash a thousand kids behind a juniper bush.

The Secretary hummed and grumbled to himself as he pressed buttons on his handheld. "My program," he remarked, "tells me that you lied or prevaricated eighty-nine times."

They rattled through an old rail yard. A few packet cars stood abandoned there, wreathed in vines, their sides all but black with rust. Packet cars! Martin scanned them avidly.

The Secretary's massive fist came down with a crash and broke the little stowaway table. "You will look at me when I'm talking to you! Ursula! Persuade Mr. Glass of the error of his ways."

But at that second, Martin spied a packet car swathed in a gray tarp. He knew that tarp! It was Rudy's. And underneath—

He bolted to his feet. "Chip, we gotta go!" he called.

"Ursula! Break something," the Secretary said. "Teach Mr. Glass some manners."

The Ursulas stood shoulder-to-shoulder in the back half of

the packet car, a fearsome barricade between Martin and the door.

"Wha—Break? What are you supposed to break?" he asked.

They gazed at him sorrowfully, as if he were a cake that had fallen in the middle. "We start with the fingers," they said.

"Don't hurt me," he begged, clutching his fingers together. "I just need to get past."

"Go ahead," the Ursulas told him.

Martin hesitated. Maybe they intended to attack him when he came within reach. But the Secretary's face flushed light purple.

"Ursula, what are you waiting for?" he roared. "Since when do you not do what I say?"

"One of us thinks hurting this boy isn't guarding the President. Guarding the President is what we're supposed to do."

"What do you mean, one of you? Which one?" Veins stood out on the Secretary's forehead. "Good Lord, he isn't one of you! That's a dog!"

The packet climbed up a long ramp. The clack of the rails grew very loud. They drowned out the Ursulas' reply.

Martin squeezed through the crowd of bots. "Come on, Chip, we're going," he called. Behind him, he heard the Secretary rage, and the crash of more broken furniture.

"Count yourselves, you idiots! You're the twelve Ursulas. There can't be thirteen of you!"

Martin flung open the door at the back of the packet. They were on a long bridge at least fifteen feet in the air, and a rush of wind whistled by the open railing. The platform was nothing but a few square feet of metal mesh. He could see straight through it, and through the open slats of the railway bridge beneath. Metal fencing zigzagged underneath the car, jagged posts, broken glass.

Chip dashed past him out onto the platform and crouched down close to the mesh. The wind turned his black fur over in waves, revealing his creamy undercoat. Martin grabbed the rail, pulled himself out, and slammed the door shut behind him. Then he froze, clinging to it as the wind buffeted him, watching the ground rush by under his feet.

"Chip," he cried, "we can't get down from here!"

CHAPTER FOURTEEN

When Martin was eight, David had dared him to put his hands in the air while they rode home on Dad's scooter. As soon as he had tried, the street had banged into him with swift and impersonal force. Martin still remembered the close-up view of the asphalt as he rolled to the curb. The street had sanded patches off his shirt and jeans. Off his hands and face as well.

But now, the Secretary of State would soon be at the door, with a new plan for dealing with his prisoners. Martin gulped. "We gotta do it. We gotta jump."

Balancing precariously, he knelt down next to his dog. Chip put his big ears back and licked Martin's face.

"Listen," Martin said, "remember William and Sim? Remember the typewriter? I need you to think like a bot and get us off of here. Not like a dog. Like a bot!"

The German shepherd snuggled close to Martin. Then he turned his shaggy head away. Handles jutted out of his neck.

"Okay, I get it." Martin scrambled astride the furry form and gripped the handles. "Just like riding a bike," he whispered, and he closed his eyes as tightly as he could.

They launched out into space.

Martin felt the exact second when they stopped moving entirely, hanging in the air like birds. Then they dropped so fast that Martin's stomach stayed behind. Now the pavement in my face, he thought, now the scrapes and scratches all over my body. He buried his face in Chip's tickly fur.

He felt them hit the ground, but they hit it in slow motion, the moment of impact elongating like a rubber band. Martin's knees touched dirt with a gentle tap. What's going on? he wondered.

Then they shot back into the air.

Martin opened his eyes. They were rising above a wide, flat space covered with faded steel hulks half-buried in cheerful yellow sunflowers. Then came the instant when they hung in the air and the stomach flop of the drop. Then they came down into the waist-high sunflowers. Then they sprang up again.

Chip hopped across row after row of the hulks like a giant pogo stick. Then he bounced in place a few times, and Martin slid off into the sunflowers' stiff green stems and fuzzy, itchy leaves.

The packet bridge that bounded one edge of the sunflower field was empty. The Secretary's car was out of sight. Martin thought he could still make out the clack of its progress in the distance, but soon the breeze sighing through the sunflowers was all he heard.

He sat right where he was, shaking all over, and put his arms around his knees and rocked. When he had been very small, rocking like this had calmed him down. Things had happened too quickly in the packet car for him to feel the danger he was in. Now that he could look back on it, he thought he might pass out.

"He was gonna have them break me up," he groaned to Chip. His fingers hurt at the thought, and then the skin on his arms and legs began to crawl. He rubbed them to cancel out the prickling sensation. The sunflowers hid him from view, and he wanted to stay hidden. He would have liked to dig a hole and crawl inside.

"The Ursulas were nice," he muttered. "You could tell they didn't wanna be mean. But *that* guy! That—that *guy*—" Martin couldn't think of a word evil enough to describe him. "He didn't just wanna kill, he acted like it didn't matter. He made out like it was a business or something!"

Chip didn't seem to share Martin's fear, or perhaps he was celebrating his emancipation from the ranks of the twelve Ursulas. He cavorted through the yellow flowers, then pounced. Seconds later, he came prancing up to Martin with a stick.

"You sure saved the day," Martin told him, "being an Ursula and all. And that jump! Wow! My legs are like jelly. That might be fun to try again sometime."

Chip sidled into Martin, knocking him off balance, and whipped his bushy tail back and forth. Yellow petals went flying like confetti.

Martin climbed to his feet and tossed the stick. Chip sped after it, muscles rippling beneath his magnificent coat. "You're a good boy," Martin told him when he returned. "You're a great dog." He tossed the stick again, and Chip sped away. "We better get going. We need to find Cassie and get help for Mom. And what if that guy comes back? Maybe he's figured out a way to make the Ursulas not listen to you."

About a mile from them, a cluster of thin buildings reached improbable heights, as if some giant hand had come down from the sky and pulled them toward the heavens. Some were faced with polished stone, still stylish and dignified. Others were faced with panels of mirrored glass. These had shattered and left dark squares here and there, so that their sides looked like surreal chessboards. Flocks of birds swooped in and out of them and gave their solid lines the illusion of movement.

"We were closer to those tall places when we saw the red packet car," Martin said. "Let's go that way."

They started toward the high buildings. Martin walked through the rows of short metal hulks, stepped over a low spot in the sagging chain-link fence that bordered them, and headed down a crumbling street. Chip snagged his stick in the rusted fence and had to leave it behind.

The sun rose higher and changed color from bright orange to white. The air heated up. Slowly, carefully, Martin and his dog threaded their way among the gigantic buildings, which towered over him, ominous and silent. Surely humans hadn't lived in such unnatural places. He couldn't imagine having the courage to go inside them, much less climb to their top floors.

The narrow streets between them were clogged with debris, some of it several feet deep. Jagged sheets of window glass sparkled in the sun like diamonds. In the shade, they turned all but invisible. A piece of glass sliced through the bottom of Martin's sneaker and barely missed drawing blood.

"Maybe this wasn't the way to come," Martin worried. "Little kids couldn't make it through all this trash. Maybe that wasn't Rudy's packet car after all. We need to find it and make sure."

But Martin was accustomed to seeing a horizon. He wasn't prepared for city streets. The collection of buildings around him seemed to shift and change as he passed them. He couldn't recognize which buildings he had walked by or which streets he had just crossed. He couldn't find his way back to the packet line.

And all the time, as he wiped the sweat that trickled into his eyes, he thought about water. He tried not to think about how thirsty he was, but he couldn't help himself. Before long, it was the only thing he could think of.

"My head hurts," he said as they plowed their way through a dim alley between two towering ruins. In spite of the hot day, the air in the alley felt clammy. Rotting, moldy trash squelched underfoot. "I don't know where the Wonder Babies have gotten to. This place is way bigger than I thought."

They turned a corner and came back out into the sunshine. Martin kicked hardened debris off a step and sat down. "My head hurts, Chip," he said again. "I'm dizzy. It's so bright out here. I don't know where we're going anymore."

They walked for hours, turning down one street after another, but they never seemed to get anywhere. The same buildings turned up in front of them again and again. We're going in circles, Martin thought, but he was too dazed to decide what to do about it. He didn't know where the Wonder Babies were, so it didn't seem to matter which way he went.

As the morning turned into afternoon, the downtown streets turned into a furnace. Shifting waves of heat radiated off the concrete and glass, and the hot, muggy breeze seemed to smother him. Martin stumbled blindly. It occurred to him that he might die.

"I don't think we're gonna find anybody," he muttered.

Chip pointed his muzzle skyward and emitted an eloquent, pitiful howl. It went on and on, the cry of a lost dog in desperate need of help. Martin joined it, yelling as loud as his roughened throat could manage. "Theo! Rudy! Help! Where are you guys?"

As the white sun crept across the concrete-colored sky, Martin staggered along the city streets, yelling for his friends. The heat deepened and took possession of everything until it seemed to Martin that he was drowning under boiling water. His hoarse voice echoed inside his aching head. He wasn't sure the yell had words, but it didn't seem to matter anymore.

A figure detached itself from the shadow of a nearby building. Chip burst into a joyful chorus and bounced ahead. Martin stumbled after him, trying to make out what it was, but his eyes had given up focusing.

It was Theo. She caught him by his sunburned arms. "We thought we heard someone calling my name," she said. "Martin, you found us again."

CHAPTER FIFTEEN

Theo led him across packed dirt, over broken bricks, and into the dark interior of a building. She turned on a flashlight and took him to a set of concrete stairs. Martin's eyes couldn't follow the flashlight's beam. He stumbled and went sprawling. He felt her pull him to his feet, drape his arm around her neck, and more or less drag him along. She was talking, but the words went by too fast for him to catch much of their meaning. "You're hot," she said at one point. "Like fire."

The next thing Martin knew, he was lying on something soft. Flashlights came and shone down on him, and a sopping sheet dropped onto him with a slapping sound. Ice tumbled down on him in a roar like thunder, and he moaned against the cold. A whimper answered him, and Chip licked his face.

For the longest time, Martin was convinced that he had fallen into the fridge and been taken prisoner by its inhabitants. Lurid dreams gripped him, in which a ketchup bottle had morphed into the evil Red Queen. She held him down and poured water into his mouth to try to drown him. He sputtered and hacked and shoved her away.

"Don't spit it all over me," Theo's voice complained. "If you weren't ready to drink it, why did you yell for it?"

"Theo!" Martin opened his eyes. "Is that you? I thought you were the ketchup!"

"That's nice. What did you get to be, the jar of pickles?"

Martin closed his eyes again and plucked at the wet sheet. "You were squeezable," he whispered.

"So I've been told."

Some time later, he woke up. The ice was gone. He was on a pallet in a small, shadowy room crammed with boxes and supplies. A flashlight lying nearby illuminated the sleeping form of Theo pillowed against a mound of blankets.

Chip was resting a few feet away. When he saw Martin move, he lifted his head and wagged. Theo opened her eyes and leaned over to feel Martin's arm.

"Your temperature's down," she muttered. "About time!"

"I'm cold," he complained, running his hand across the thin sheet that covered him. "Can I have a blanket?"

"You've got a blanket," she said as she checked the contents of a plastic bag dangling above his head. "That's a medical blanket there. It knows exactly what you need. Right now, you need thin and light, so it's thin and light."

"But that's not what I want," Martin protested, plucking at it. He squinted through the gloom at the plastic bag she was looking at and discovered that it connected to him via a tube in his arm. "Ugh! There's a line in me. Take it out!"

Theo smiled. "When this bag is empty," she said. "Be glad it's there. It probably saved your life."

"Can't I just drink it?"

"Judging from the stuff you spit up on me—no."

Martin went back to sleep.

When he woke up again, Theo was gone, and Chip lay curled up across his legs. A slender person was rummaging through a cardboard box across the room from him. She set it aside with an irritated sigh and swung her flashlight in search of another, and the white beam illuminated her face.

"William!" Martin said. He scrambled to sit up, acutely aware of his lack of clothes. The medical blanket, sensing the spike in his blood pressure, promptly shredded into a panel of mesh. "More fluff! More fluff!" he whispered frantically, and, to his relief, it obeyed.

He needn't have worried. William continued her search without turning around. "Hello," she said. "Feeling better, I see."

She must have eyes in the back of her head, Martin thought.

"I had a plastic tube in my arm," he told her. It was gone now, he noticed as he poked the bandage. How had he not woken up for that?

"Intravenous cannula," she said. "Theo used two of our bags of saline on you, not to mention the ice that was supposed to keep the milk from going bad."

William slammed the second box aside, picked up her flashlight, and started digging through another box.

"What are you looking for?" Martin asked.

"Antiemesis drugs," she said. "Here they are." She pulled out several foil packets. "My three-year-olds are vomiting. They threw up all over me."

Now that she mentioned it, Martin could tell even in that dim light that she wasn't at her best. Her hair fell in untidy strings around her face, and her tense silhouette spoke of frustration and lack of sleep.

"I think I threw up on Theo," Martin said. In retrospect, this didn't sound like the sort of comment likely to produce a bond, but he couldn't think of anything that would.

William shoved the boxes back into place and held her flashlight close so she could read the directions on the foil packet.

"Sorry about the milk going bad," Martin said.

"It doesn't matter," she murmured. "It isn't as if there was a lot to begin with. Of milk, or of anything else."

Martin pondered this. "Why don't you steal some more?"

"We can't," William snapped. "They're watching the big shipments to catch us stealing again. They were watching them before; we found out that's how they were zeroing in on us. If Central gets a hint of which direction we've gone, they'll be crawling all over this city inch by inch."

"Okay, I get it. You don't have to yell. And if that's how things are, you might want to hide the red packet car a little better. I spotted it right off."

He was almost sorry he'd said this. William looked more exhausted than before. "That's just great," she muttered. "I'll get word to Rudy." And she collected her foil packets and walked out.

The next time Martin woke up, Theo was there again.

"For breakfast, you can have juice and pudding, or pudding and juice," she said. Anticipating his reply, she peeled back the foil top on a pudding cup.

Martin remembered what William had told him. "Maybe I better just skip it."

Theo frowned and handed him the cup. "Eat your breakfast!" So Martin went to work on the vanilla pudding.

"How do you feel?" she asked.

"Kind of awful. But I have to talk to you and Rudy," he said. "My mom's in trouble. We need help."

"Rudy wants to talk to you, too," she said. "When you're done, you can put your clothes on, and we'll go find him." She handed him a juice pack.

"You don't have much food left," Martin protested.

"What does that have to do with you needing juice?" So Martin took the juice, too.

Once his meal was over, she gave him his clothes. It was just as well she'd waited. His jeans and T-shirt hadn't been washed since he'd left Suburb HM1, and a robust odor emanated from them, not unlike the smell of the mattress full of mice he and Dad had expelled from their new home. Theo tried to shake the clothes out, but that only seemed to encourage the aroma.

"I'll be outside," she said as she handed them over. "Hey, they could be worse."

"Yeah, I know. I've seen William."

Martin stood up to pull on his jeans. The medical blanket came with him. He gave it a quick tug, but it clung to him.

"Look," he said, "I don't need you now. I'm all fine again. Maybe you think I'll get cold, but it's okay, I've got clothes." He pulled on his jeans. "See? Let go."

But the blanket didn't let go.

He tried to loosen its fleecy grip. He grabbed one side and pulled hard, but the blanket stretched like chewing gum. Then it brought two corners together below his chin and tied them in a square knot.

"What the hey—"

Martin pulled his T-shirt over the top of the blanket, but it shrank, wriggled through the neck hole, and settled around his shoulders like a superhero cape.

"Chip, do you think you can talk sense into this thing?"

Chip tried. He came up close and vibrated. Then he sat back and wagged apologetically. The blanket refused to budge. Martin held out his arms and surveyed his new accessory. All these years, he'd been irrationally attached to his clothing, but he'd never imagined that a piece of clothing might become irrationally attached to him.

"Never mind, Chip," he said. "I don't think it's gonna change its mind."

Theo was waiting for him outside the door. Chip lit his eyebeams, and the three of them made their way through a dark labyrinth of passages. Martin couldn't make sense of his surroundings. The space was as gloomy as the underworld of HM1, but it was broken up into wide hallways and big rooms. It couldn't be a house, Martin thought. No family could have lived in a building like this.

Groups of little children huddled in the corners under the supervision of weary teachers. The children's small white faces shimmered in the flashlight beams and reminded Martin of ghosts. He looked for Cassie, but he didn't spot her or her friends.

The place was dank and dirty. Broken metal straps poked out from the walls and threatened to jab Martin in the eye. Dust and insect webbing cocooned ancient plastic chairs and tables, and some corridors they passed were choked with garbage. The smell of mildew permeated everything.

Children shouldn't be in here, Martin thought. It's not safe.

"This place looks like a game of House-to-House," he said unhappily.

"Let's hope it doesn't come to that," Theo said. "We're in the bottom of a big general-purpose building. It was the biggest basement we could find, and since the building doesn't go up too high, we're hoping it won't fall down while we're here."

"How long will that be?" Martin asked.

Theo sighed. "As long as it takes."

"I can hear kids crying. Is Cassie okay?"

"I think so. As okay as the rest of us."

They came through a doorway into a room lit to stark brilliance by two big emergency lights. Half a dozen of the prototypes were there, bending over handhelds or tuning machinery. William sat on a folding chair with a cup of coffee in her hand. She looked very tired.

Rudy came over to greet him. The handsome young man who ran the Wonder Baby school still looked dynamic, even in a wrinkled T-shirt. "I'm glad to see you looking so much better," he said. Martin didn't remember having seen him earlier. He wondered if Rudy had played a part in his ketchup-bottle delirium.

Rudy waved him to a seat, and the prototypes pulled their chairs into a ragged circle around him. He noticed William eying his blanket cape and felt a blush warm his cheeks. The blanket obligingly ventilated itself into a charming panel of lace.

"Thank you for alerting us to the danger of the red packet," Rudy said. "I knew it was too conspicuous, but we've faced so many problems in the last forty-eight hours that we haven't been able to do anything about it. I'm glad to see you again, but you may be sorry you've joined us. Central is closing in fast, and I'm afraid we're out of options."

"I'm really sorry about that," Martin said. "See, I came here to ask for help." He described Mom's strange illness. "At least can you tell me what's wrong with her?"

"It's an old identity microchip," Theo said. "She's about thirty-five, isn't she? Maybe a little older."

"The last of the identity chips," Rudy agreed. "They started out as standard issue, but no one ever went outside the domes, so they seemed like a waste of money after a while. They were phased out in the seventies, but for a few years, the lab was still putting them in about a quarter of the newborns. Your dad seems to be fine, but I'm afraid your mom had the bad luck to get one."

"What does it do?"

"It's transmitting. Those chips stay quiet in the suburbs or in the game show complex because they stay in touch with a base transponder. A set number of days after the chip goes out of range, it begins to transmit at an amplified volume. Each time its host moves, it transmits its new location. Your mom is fine as long as she stays still, but when she moves, it transmits, and that interferes with the functioning of her brain."

Martin felt as if he were suffocating, and the room tilted and spun. "But you can fix her, right? I mean, I broke her by bringing her out there, but it's not forever because someone can fix her—right? Because she can't stay like that, with something wrong in her brain. She can't stay like that!"

"Sure, we can fix her," Theo said. "Don't worry, Martin. Those chips aren't too hard to knock out. I can go do it, Rudy. I know the town he's talking about."

"It's risky," Rudy said.

"Oh, I don't think so. Who bothers to listen to those old frequencies these days? If they did listen in, she'll be gone by the time I get there, and I'll just turn around and come back."

Martin's heart was pounding. "But you can't leave, Theo. What about Cassie? She's in trouble too! You gotta fix this."

Rudy paused. Then he gave an encouraging smile. "That's where maybe *you* can help us."

Martin could see what was coming. It all fell into place. He was caught, trapped, just like Mom and Cassie were trapped. None of them had a choice.

"You wanna mess with my dog."

Rudy nodded.

"Listen, is this even gonna matter?" Martin asked. "How do you think Chip's gonna help?"

Rudy leaned forward in his folding chair and laid a hand on Chip's ruff. Chip rolled a nervous eye at Martin. "Honestly, I don't know," Rudy said. "William has some theories. But you've seen the influence Chip has had on bots, even bots with high security clearance. And the fact is, we don't have anything else to try. In another couple of days—Well, never mind. Let's just say that the situation is critical."

In another couple of days, Martin thought, the Wonder Babies will start dying. They don't have enough to eat or drink, and they're already getting sick. Jimmy, baby Laura . . . Cassie, too. In a week, my little sister might be dead.

He swallowed the lump in his throat. "What do you need to do to Chip?"

"We'll look at his boards," William said. "And then we'll—"

"No, you won't," Theo interrupted. "You'll take him to

Malcolm. You know it's the right thing to do. With a little luck, you can get there and back in a day. The school can survive that long."

William's eyes lit up. She noticed Martin looking at her, and a blush crept across her pale cheeks. She said, "Malcolm Granville knows more about bots than anyone else in the world."

But Rudy was frowning. He stopped petting Chip and straightened up. "Why Malcolm?" he said. "You think we can't handle this ourselves?"

Theo stared him down. Martin hadn't seen her look so serious before. It was as if the rest of them had vanished, and only she and Rudy were in the room.

"I think you need Malcolm's advice," she said. "About the bot, and about other things too. Before this is over, you should hear what he has to say."

"I'm not dragging my oldest friend into this," Rudy said stubbornly.

"If I know Malcolm, he's already in it," Theo said. "Do this for me, Rudy, if you won't do it for yourself. And take William with you. See if he'll keep her there."

Martin felt weak and dizzy. His head was starting to pound. "What are you people talking about?" he cried. "What does this have to do with my dog?"

"I'm sorry, Martin," Rudy said. "Theo thinks we should take your bot to Dr. Malcolm Granville, the head of the Robotics and Intelligent Systems Laboratory. She's right; if anyone can, Malcolm will know how to make Chip function properly."

"He does function properly," Martin whispered.

Rudy's handsome face was earnest and sympathetic. "I know this is hard for you," he said. "I wish we had another choice. But I know you want to help your sister, and this is the best thing to try. I won't ask you to do the wrong thing, I promise. I need you to trust me."

Martin swallowed. Then he nodded.

"Okay. I trust you. Chip, we're gonna go find out what you are."

CHAPTER SIXTEEN

The meeting broke up. Theo had Martin describe the house she was looking for. "I'll tell your mom hello," she said, tousling his dirty hair. Then she enveloped Rudy in a big bear hug.

She's saying good-bye, Martin thought. She doesn't think she'll see him again.

Rudy told William to find some clean clothes for Martin and herself, as well as put together some supplies. Martin staggered after her, so tired that he could barely stay on his feet. "I think I can get us a gallon of water to wash in," she said. "You look bad. I'll get you one of our energy drinks." Martin wondered if she was being sympathetic or sarcastic.

Not long afterward, the two of them were peeking out a rubble-choked exit at the rosy light of dawn outside. Quick footsteps behind them announced Rudy's arrival. He was wearing a crumpled brown sport coat and trousers, and he carried an attaché case. "William, you had to settle for jeans, I see."

William wrinkled up her nose. "All the T-shirts were too short to be dresses."

"Chip looks great, as usual," Rudy said with a smile. "And, Martin, you cleaned up pretty well. Still got the medical blanket. That's a smart idea. You never know when you'll need it."

"It isn't that," Martin explained as he followed Rudy through the opening. "It's just that I can't get it to go away."

Rudy laughed. "You must be the perfect patient."

The sun had barely risen by the time they reached the packet rails. Rudy dug into a drift of trash and soil beside a tar-smeared rail tie and found a small metal cube. Its cover flipped back to reveal an outlet. He produced a battered orange box with a short wire from his attaché case and pushed the wire into the cube.

A small panel on the orange box lit up:

A▓AILABLE OP▓IONS:
S▓OP E▓STBOUN▓
▓TOP ▓EST▓OUND
PRE▓▓ BUTTON ▓N▓ SPEA▓

Rudy held down the large gray button below the panel.

"Stop westbound," he ordered.

The panel responded:

▓TO▓ WEST▓OUN▓

And it began to blink.

"Can't we take the red packet?" Martin asked. "Or will they be looking for it?"

"We have to pass cameras," Rudy said. "I think they'd spot it. Now we wait, but we need to wait out of sight." And he led them a few feet away to crouch behind an odd section of solitary wall. "I checked the schedules. We've got a possible carrier coming through at seven thirty and another at ten after nine. We won't know if they'll work until one of them stops. This box only works on a certain kind of car."

"What kind?" Martin asked.

"That's right, you're a packet chief's son," Rudy said. "Maybe you know about these cars. In the early days of the steel domes, the packet chiefs didn't have bots to do their work, so they and their crews used these boxes to go out and work on the lines. The old engineers, the packet drivers, had just been replaced with artificial intelligence engines. These cars still have a seat and a window in the front where the engineer used to sit."

"I've seen cars like that," Martin said. "They're really scruffy. Trash trucks, cement mixers, stuff like that."

"That's the kind. This morning sends a gravel car and a chicken hauler our way. We'll see how lucky we get."

Rudy gazed at the rails with an unreadable expression on his face. When he noticed Martin watching him, he roused himself and smiled. Martin remembered Cassie saying that the head of the Wonder Baby school tried to keep the little children from worrying.

That's how I wanna be, Martin thought with a surge of admiration. He's so smart he's like a superhero, but he acts like it's no big deal.

The sun crept up the sky, and birds began to fly overhead. Chip sniffed around in the dirt. Martin watched his dog with an uneasy feeling in his stomach. William was watching Chip too.

"Can you tell us about your bot?" she asked. "We should learn as much as we can." So Martin told them every extraordinary thing he could remember his pet doing. Bragging turned out to be a bittersweet pleasure.

"So, what do you hope Chip turns out to be?" he asked. "What's he gonna do to save the Wonder Babies?"

William plucked a nearby wildflower and began stripping off its stiff leaves.

"He's probably a very high-ranking military bot," she said. "He gave orders to the freight bots, and to a military officer bot . . . even to all twelve Ursulas at once. That means he may be able to command an entire battalion of soldiers, and then we could use them to fight for us."

Chip dug into the dirt to find a cool patch of ground. Then he lay down on the sandy earth with a sigh.

"I dunno," Martin said. "He doesn't seem very military to me. Sure, he talks to bots, but it's not like he orders them around. And he felt really bad when he had to kill those three wild dogs."

William's brows knit together into a scowl. "The toy chips in him are blocking his potential."

"Maybe," Rudy said. "Or maybe he's confused about his canine identity, and he tried to apply the sanctity-of-life clause to dogs as well as humans. Bots aren't supposed to kill humans without special orders. Maybe he thought he shouldn't kill a dog, either."

"If he isn't military," William said, "then he might be a very expensive modified bot, something a criminal gang ordered up. The most powerful modified bots can turn into one-machine armies. They can bring down every computer within miles, and that includes the computers on weapons and guided missiles. We could jam Central's spying bugs, and they wouldn't know which way we went."

"Like a bot superhero," Martin said. "I kinda like that. Chip, are you a one-bot army?"

Chip rose, rooted around in his bed of cool dirt, and sneezed explosively. Then he wagged at Martin.

"Chip has the right idea," Rudy said. "This kind of speculation is pointless until we get to Malcolm. He'll be able to tell us what's going on."

A jackrabbit sped by them, and Chip jumped to his feet to chase it. William got up and walked back and forth, squinting at the sun. Martin discovered a sandy cone of the sort that held the wonderful bug he'd found before, and he dug out its inhabitant to show William.

"It's in the family Myrmeleontidae," she told him. "Order Neuroptera. They eat ants. They grow up into winged insects like a little dragonfly, with clavate antennae and four transparent, similarly shaped wings."

Martin shook the soft bug back onto the ground. "I just like how they scoot backward," he said.

"Almost time," Rudy called. "I should warn you two"—Chip trotted up with a piece of broken board—"that is, I should warn you three. This AI won't be very nice."

"Not nice?" William echoed, puzzled.

"No. To put the AI together, they took scans of an old packet car engineer. He was pretty upset about being replaced by a machine, and it comes through the AI."

With a squeal of brakes, a hopper car stopped by the orange box. "Get inside," Rudy told them.

Martin ran up to the packet and pulled open a narrow door at the front. An ancient bench ran across its width, covered in crackled mushroom-colored vinyl. In front of the bench was a panel of gauges and controls. Over the panel's top arched a sloping glass window.

"Get in! Get in!" Rudy yelled.

William climbed into the cabin. When she sat down on the vinyl seat, it disintegrated in a puff of cheddar-colored dust. Martin climbed in behind her. Next came Chip, hampered by his efforts to bring his broken board along. When Rudy saw them all safely inside, he pulled the orange box from its receptacle and threw himself in after them. By the time he pulled the door shut, the packet was already accelerating.

"Good work!" Rudy said. He hunted among the gauges, located another metal cover, and plugged the orange box into the outlet underneath. The box turned into a speaker, and the members of the boarding party discovered that the AI was already talking.

"Useless brats!" it fumed. "A waste of perfectly good oxygen that could be used in fuel combustion. I guess you think it's some great dream of mine to haul your butts around. Well, guess what? You're wrong!"

"We appreciate your stopping for us—," Rudy began.

"Like I had a choice!" the AI yelled.

"—and we'd like to know if you'll be passing Branch Line 185."

"What am I, your Magic Eight-Ball?" the AI snapped. *"Ask again later."*

"What's he talking about?" Martin muttered to William. William gave a shrug.

Rudy blew out his breath in a sigh. Then he tried again.

"Today's schedule tells me you pass Branch Line 185. Please stop and let us out at that junction. If the schedule is incorrect, and you aren't passing there, please take us as close as you can."

"'Take us as close as you can,'" whined the AI. "As if I don't already have a job involving a very important batch of gravel that needs to reach its destination as soon as possible! 'Take us around the country, Mr. AI. Show us all the sites.' The only place you're going to is the bottom of a hole, and the only thing you'll see there is sixteen cubic yards of crushed limestone aggregate pouring down out of the sky!"

Chip leaned forward and vibrated at the orange box. The AI subsided.

"Nobody told me I had a rail yard engineer on board. It's good to meet an old-timer. I used to work Roseville, myself. We'll be passing BL 185 around fourteen thirty, and I'll stop and let you off. I hope that helps."

"That sounds perfect," Rudy said.

"Stick a sock in it!" snapped the AI. "I'm doing this for the engineer, not you gas-exchanging carbon-based bacteria breeding farms. I better not hear another word."

For a long time, they obeyed him. The scenery shifted and changed. They passed mountains, then flat fields covered with waist-high grass that bent in silvery swaths before the wind. Martin craned his neck to catch every detail as the vast land rolled by.

Chip was in the way. He was too big for the narrow seat. He sat bolt upright for a while, but his piece of board kept bumping into Martin's head. Then he tried to lie down, but there wasn't any room. At last, he clambered into Martin's lap and curled up as tightly as he could. His pointy elbows dug into Martin's thigh and sent Martin's leg to sleep almost instantly. His back end overflowed onto Rudy, and his board poked William in the ribs. As he gnawed the board, shavings and splinters showered down onto William's jeans.

While Chip chewed, Martin poked patterns into the dog's thick, fuzzy coat, smoothing out cones like the houses of the little backward-scooting bugs. I may not get to do this again, he thought unhappily. His mind sent him pictures of a future Chip, turned into some blank-faced soldier bot. He shook them off. Rudy says to trust him, he thought. I'll trust him. I won't worry about this.

But he couldn't stop himself from feeling miserable.

They passed through several abandoned cities huddled by the rails, as unnatural and decayed as corpses. Off in the distance, steel domes winked at them from distant hills. They shared a silent lunch of oatmeal bars, and Rudy made Martin drink the rest of their water.

Around one o'clock, they came to an empty rail yard with forty or fifty sets of rails laid out in parallel lines. Only a few packet cars remained in this mighty outdoor loading bay. Their paint had gone long ago, and they were so old, they looked like part of the landscape.

"I used to work this yard," the AI announced gruffly. "God, what a place it was: men yelling, cars crashing and screeching . . . and the stink! We'd have a hundred cattle cars sitting in the sun; the damn racket just about drove you around the bend. And now look at it, all gone to hell." They rolled past silent loading cranes. "Some lame, pathetic, boneheaded future this has turned out to be."

Martin fell asleep to the rhythmic clicking of the rails and the gentle side-to-side motion of the car. When he woke up, the land had turned pink.

He peered out the bug-smeared front window. They were chugging through a small hollow among short hills of light pink rock that flowed in scoops and mounds, rose into odd pinnacles, and tumbled off into piles of boulders. Across the pink ground ranged desert scrub punctuated by pale, fuzzy cholla and twisted piñon pines. As they rolled along, the jumbled scenery swung around them, revealing new gullies and hiding entire hills behind a rock or two. The whole landscape felt as if it were in motion.

"Wow!" Martin breathed.

"We're getting close," Rudy whispered. "Wake up William."

A cluster of emerald green towers rose out of the pink landscape in front of them, smooth and sparkling and altogether wonderful. The dark, sleek skyscrapers were such a fanciful addition to the scenery that they looked like something from a dream.

Ahead, Martin could see a Y in the packet line. A line snaked off to the left, toward the sparkling green buildings. "Leave us off here," Rudy commanded. "Chip?" And Chip vibrated a repetition of the command.

"Good riddance!" shouted the AI.

They climbed out of the hopper car into the blistering heat of a desert afternoon, and their packet clattered away. Within seconds, it was hidden by a fold in the land. Soon, not even the sound remained.

Martin didn't want to say so, but the emerald skyscrapers seemed very far away. The enervating heat and his drowsiness made him want to lie down right where he was and bake on a rock like a lizard. "Gonna take us a couple of hours to walk that," he muttered to William.

William was busy trying to brush the bright orange dust of the bench from her clothing. She squinted at their destination. "Five minutes, tops."

Rudy set down his attaché case and pulled out his lab coat. He put it on and smoothed the most obvious wrinkles. "Now, don't use any names once we get inside," he cautioned. "They'll get picked up by the bugs and trigger alerts at Central. Don't use the words 'prototype' or 'Wonder Babies,' either. If we can finish our business with Malcolm in less than an hour, we should be able to make it out before they catch us."

Then he cupped his hands around his mouth and yelled toward the faraway skyscrapers.

"Malcolm! Hey, Malcolm! It's me!"

Within seconds, a dot appeared on the thread of distant track in front of the green glass spires and gained size rapidly as it whizzed toward them. It turned out to be a small open-air packet car rolling backward. Two fantastical park benches spanned its narrow width. It shuddered to a stop right in front of them.

"Hold on tight," Rudy advised as they climbed aboard. "Malcolm likes speed. And surprises."

The little car accelerated dramatically. Soon, they were bouncing up and down with jaw-breaking intensity as the wind blew into their faces. William's hair flew everywhere, and she couldn't let go long enough to get it out of her eyes. Martin was terrified, but once the car slowed down, he wished it would speed up again.

The car rolled beneath an archway in the first huge green building. It came to a stop in a charming foyer floored with dark gray-green stonework and walled by impressively large panels of glass. The cool touch of climate-controlled air flowed past them, and yet they still seemed to be outside; the sun shone through in sparkling beams and cast the shadow of their packet car onto the floor. But the light that entered here wasn't plain outdoor light. It was rarified and golden. It made everything seem shiny and beautiful, even the packet rails, which ended a few feet ahead of them in an ornate blockade of curving and curling brasswork.

Martin stood up, then promptly sat back down. His blanket had stretched itself through the holes in the park bench and wrapped him up like a ham sandwich in a baggie. "Okay, okay, we're stopped," he said, tugging at it. "I get it, you don't like speed. You didn't have to come with me, you know."

The blanket uncurled itself from the bench, fluttering with agitation.

Chip hopped down and stood next to the packet car, tall ears pricked. His black-and-tan coat seemed to glow. "You know, Chip," Martin said, "you always look great whenever we go anywhere fancy."

William climbed off the cart, trying to comb her tangled hair with her fingers. Rudy jumped down and surveyed the foyer with the eagerness of a boy. "He changes this place every time I see it."

"Over here, please!"

Beside them, between the packet lines and the wall, stood a long counter of dark marbled wood with a black granite countertop. Behind the counter, a slender woman beckoned them with long, fine hands. Her pale hair was twined into an elaborate mass of ringlets around her cat-shaped face, and her slanted eyes were impossibly large and green. All in all, she looked a little too much like a praying mantis in a wig.

"Please," she called again, rapping on the countertop with a pink nail, and Rudy strolled over to her.

"Welcome to the Robotics and Intelligent Systems Laboratory," the woman fluted, bending her long neck and smiling coquettishly through her ringlets. She was wearing a pink blouse that looked like spun cotton candy, and every fragile bone in her upper body appeared to be half as thick as normal, and almost twice as long.

I hope she doesn't try to shake hands, Martin thought. No way can I go through with it. She's the scariest thing I've seen.

"Sir, your visit is a delightful surprise," cooed the mantis lady to Rudy, looking down and tapping with her long fingernails on something out of sight. Martin glanced over the high granite counter and discovered a further countertop below, along with what looked like the casing of a computer console tilted so that only the mantis lady could read it. "Although, I'm told that for this visit, you're Dr. Donner Chapel." She gave a tinkling laugh. "I'm sure I don't know why."

Rudy smiled. "One of Malcolm's little jokes."

She laughed again and shook a long finger at Rudy as if he'd been rude. Martin's blanket patted sweat from his forehead.

She wasn't a real woman, was she? Could a real woman have fingers eight inches long?

"Dr. Granville is at work in a sterilized room at the moment," she trilled, "so your path will take you to the patio garden for light refreshments. After you've had a few minutes to recover from your journey, your path heads up to the top floor of the executive tower, where you will meet with Dr. Granville in his office. I hope that will be satisfactory."

"That sounds fine."

"Then . . ." She spread her elongated hands wide. Very wide. "In that case, your path awaits."

Her icing pink fingernail pointed to an Oriental rug by their feet. A shiny brass banister closed off its far end. Martin had assumed that the rail marked where people should line up to talk to her. On closer inspection, the rail appeared to be attached to the carpet itself.

"A path, eh?" Rudy said. "That's new."

Once they were on it, the carpet shook itself and rose infinitesimally into the air. Then it lurched forward. Martin's blanket reached around him and hitched itself to the brass rail to prevent him from tumbling off.

"You fabric things!" Martin groaned. "Someone should have warned me about you."

As they swept by the end of the counter, Martin glanced back at the mantis lady. She wasn't standing behind the desk in sensible shoes, and she wasn't sitting on a chair. Her torso ended at the surface of the lower countertop, and the "computer screen" she tapped at with those long fingers was a plain block of wood.

"She's not real!" he hissed to William.

"She's real," William whispered back. "She just isn't alive."

"Have a nice day," the woman called, waving her hand, as their carpet whisked them around the corner.

CHAPTER SEVENTEEN

Their path flowed up a curving incline and down broad steps into the heart of the bottle green empire. At no point was their view of the towering glass walls entirely obscured. Conventional offices might run along one side of their path, but the other was open to the sky. Walkways from office suite to office suite crossed over one another on narrow bridges high in the air.

"Is this what your lab was like?" Martin muttered to William.

"Not the part I lived in," William said.

The center of the office complex was an elaborate flower garden complete with fully grown trees, and the multistory office blocks of brown and black stone rose around it like vertical mountains. Birds flew and sang beneath the glass roof, and yellow sunbeams dripped through the thick foliage like honey.

The Oriental rug stopped in the middle of the lush greenery by a teakwood table. A small monkey in a red cap and pants swooped down and balanced on their rail.

"Please sit and share some refreshments," said the monkey in the low, measured tones of a newscaster. "I can offer you an excellent strawberry-lemonade ice, freshly squeezed and flash-frozen."

"That sounds perfect," Rudy said, and William nodded.

"How about you, sir?" the monkey asked, turning to Martin.

"Will a strawberry-lemonade ice be adequate, or would you prefer that I bring you something else?"

Martin gazed into the monkey's big brown eyes. "Um . . . the ice, please," he said.

"I'll be right back," the monkey promised, and sprang away through the trees.

Soon, Martin was sipping an incomparable slushy and admiring the flowers that grew nearby. Chip lay at his feet, eyes closed in deep relaxation. The monkey had pulled a power cable from the bushes and offered it to the dog: "To rejuvenate you, sir, our finest pulse charging system. Note the gold plating on the prongs."

Martin picked through a tray of unusual fruit and selected a star-shaped apple. The apple had no seeds at its core, only sweet white flesh with just the right amount of crisp snap. "I could get used to this," he said.

"This is the world of the high-tech labs," Rudy said. "The scientists live in luxury. Their experiments live underground and seldom see the sun. I used to eat these starpples for breakfast."

"And these walls have ears too," Martin said in a low voice.

"Yes and no. We have a lot of freedom, but when a lab is under suspicion, everything gets checked, from how our pupils dilate when we're talking about certain topics to what chemicals get thrown off in our urine."

"Ugh," Martin said, but he finished his starpple anyway. A bluebird flitted down and offered him a cluster of matching blue grapes, and he discovered that they didn't have any seeds either.

William ate a skinless orange, shiny as a gold lollipop. "No names, remember," she warned Martin.

"That's right," Rudy said. "We don't have to worry about the end-of-day analysis. We'll be gone by then. It's the big things that we have to watch out for. Names. The special nouns I told you about. Just try to keep quiet as much as possible."

Three jewel-toned dragonflies hovered over the table and began to hum in a delicate harmony. Martin's blanket took aim at the nearest one and swatted it away. The monkey dropped down onto the table again and collected their empty glasses. "I hope you've enjoyed your refreshments," it murmured. "If you would be so kind as to resume your path now."

This time, the Oriental rug took them inside a glass elevator, and they rose to the top of the tallest tower. The rug flowed down a long balcony with a dizzying view and through the door of a grand mahogany-paneled office. There, it paused long enough to let them disembark. Then it left the room with a gentle rustle.

Wide windows wrapped around three sides of the office. Martin walked along them and feasted his eyes on the view of the pink desert outside. He didn't like heights, but being here wasn't like being on Hertz's hill, maybe because he had walls and a roof to protect him. Besides, the ground was so far away that it didn't seem like ground anymore.

The packet line zigzagged and curved across the arid terrain until it crept over the uneven horizon, but that was the only sign of human life in the entire exotic landscape. All Martin could see were rocks, canyons, mounds, and arroyos sprinkled with desert plants.

Chip hopped along with his front paws on the narrow windowsill, looking out too. He left heart-shaped nose prints on the glass. Martin didn't think at first that the glass had any color to it, but then he realized that it did. The sky looked too blue, and the desert plants looked too green. The ground was the orangey pink color of Mom's tortilla warmer.

"Where are we?" Martin said. "Out here . . . this all looks really different from back near my suburb."

William was examining the contents of the shelves that occupied the remaining wall. All sorts of odds and ends cluttered them: pieces of robotic junk, odd sculptures, interesting toys. William picked up a small rag doll, and it uttered a piercing scream. She put it down again.

"We're near the coast," she said. "All the labs are out here. Close to Central, over that way." She pointed vaguely to the west.

"What's a coast?" Martin wanted to know.

The door burst open, and a young man in a lab coat strode into the room. He had a broad-shouldered, stocky build, and his black hair was cut so close to his head that it was little more than a shadow on his scalp. His skin was the color of cappuccino, and his eyes were dark olive green.

"Big brother!" he cried, coming forward to clasp Rudy's arms.

Chip shied away from the newcomer and came to sit on Martin's feet. "Hey, boy, it's okay," Martin whispered to him. But it isn't okay, he thought.

"Is he really his brother?" he muttered to William. "He's way too old to be one of the you-know-whats."

Dr. Granville overheard him.

"Yes, we're brothers," he said. "When your friend here was two years old, his designer brought him to visit the RISLab, and my father decided he had to have one like him right away. Except for a few tweaks, of course; Daddy Granville was very proud of his heritage."

"And except for a little difference in allowance," Rudy added. "Malcolm here was quite the favorite son. There I was, stuck with the other experimental subjects in the underground dormitory, with nothing to call my own but my locker and my cot. Meanwhile, Malcolm had everything money could buy and a genius in robotics could dream up. Remember that pony you got for your fifth birthday? And when I came out for the summer and we played Robin Hood, your dad made you your own merry men."

Dr. Granville laughed. "That pony had six legs. More sure-footed, and a smoother ride. How's my sweetheart?" he asked, turning to William. "You're growing older by the day and lovelier by the minute."

William didn't look older at all; in fact, she'd never looked younger. Her cheeks had brightened to the color of bubble gum. Great, thought Martin, I'm not the only one in this room who's stuck in a stupid schoolyard crush.

"Did you study those schematics I gave you?" Dr. Granville asked.

William nodded vigorously. "Every day. Until I had to leave them behind."

Dr. Granville grew serious. He clapped Rudy on the shoulder.

"I'm glad you came to me. There's news. They're reopening your lab."

Rudy's face became unreadable. "Are they?"

"Of course," Dr. Granville said. "We all knew they would once they'd punished the old scientists. It's too important a lab to lose. You can come back, and come back at the top. They're hunting you down, you know. You don't want to go back to being an experiment in your own lab."

William took a nervous step back at this idea, but Rudy put on one of his charming smiles.

"Malcolm," he said, taking Dr. Granville's arm and giving it a little shake, "you know I wouldn't put you in the middle of this. Don't forget, you have your own lab to lose! I'm only here because we have a bot problem to work out, and we'll leave as soon as we're done. I'd like you to meet a friend of mine—and his unusual pet."

"Well met," Dr. Granville said, advancing to shake Martin's hand. "I'll admit, I've heard something about you. And is this the legendary bot himself? Well, well."

He tilted his head and stared at Chip. Under his scrutiny, Chip started to pant. He circled Martin's legs nervously and sat down on his feet again. Then he looked up and gave a quick whine.

"He has a very intelligent look, doesn't he?" Dr. Granville said. "My guess is that your bot is just playing at being a dog. But the devotion is real." He glanced up at Martin again. "Good Lord, is that one of my fourth-generation medical blankets? It's turned itself into outerwear!"

Martin blushed and touched his cape, which, due to the

warm conditions, had assumed a light cotton texture. "I tried to get it to go away, but it won't."

"One problem at a time," Dr. Granville said. He crouched down in front of the anxious dog. "William, what did you learn from his board?"

"There are two boards," William said. "But I haven't seen them. His owner wouldn't let me."

Martin put a protective arm around Chip's neck. "He's scared of resets, sir."

Dr. Granville's eyebrows went up. "Retrofitted?" he mused. "Well, don't worry," he went on as he ruffled Chip's ears. "We probably won't have to reset you. But we need to see your boards, so do me a favor. You've seen glass, clear glass, like these windows here. I need you to simulate glass for me so I can get a good look at your circuits."

Chip glanced from Dr. Granville to Martin. *Should I?* his dark eyes asked.

"Go ahead," Martin told him in a low voice.

The color in Chip's gorgeous coat faded out until he looked like the silver ghost of a German shepherd. Then his rough hairs smoothed to satin. In seconds, he was a clear statue with two green circuit boards lodged in his chest.

"Very pretty!" Dr. Granville said. "But I'm seeing some distortion. Can you thin this area out? That's it; perfectly flat. Good. Very good. Now, do me a favor and don't move."

William crouched down by Dr. Granville's side and pushed her hair out of her face as she leaned forward. Rudy bent down to see too.

"Retrofitted, just as I thought," Dr. Granville announced.

"This toy board came later. See the clumsy soldering? That wasn't done in a factory. He lost consciousness as one kind of bot and woke up as another. No wonder he's afraid of resets."

Dr. Granville pulled a small lens from his pocket and fitted it over his left eye. It gave off a tiny hum as it focused. He peered closely at the boards. Then he jumped up, handed the lens to William, and sat down on the top of his desk.

"Why he's been altered is a bit of a puzzle," he said. "But there's no mystery about what he is. That's the circuit board of an elected official."

William looked crestfallen. "Are you sure?" she asked.

"Positive. There's a regular hoard of them coming out these days, and they're adding to the list all the time. Mayors, judges, county commissioners, corporation protocol officers, game show producers, you name it. Even half the talk show hosts are bots these days. No one seems to notice the difference. All in line with the favorite motto of the Savior of Our Nation: 'The best way to safeguard a democracy is to keep the people out of it.'"

"A politician." Rudy's face clouded in disappointment. "Well, that settles that."

Martin shifted uncomfortably. "It settles what?" he asked.

William peered through the lens at Chip's transparent insides. "Dr. Granville, did your people make him?"

"Oh, heavens, no," Dr. Granville replied. "They get produced in an automated facility. Never touched by human hands. William, did you note the connections? What do you make of it?"

"It couldn't be worse! The boards have been married so that

the connections can't be severed. He's always going to be a dog."

Martin's heart gave a leap. "Really?"

"Not quite," Dr. Granville cautioned. "He'll always be a dog if he wants to be."

"But I don't understand," William said. "What about his amazing skills? What about the other bots? How can he be fooling them if he's nothing but a talk show host in disguise?"

"That is a mystery," Dr. Granville conceded, "but the mystery is why, not how. See the little gray chip snapped onto the daughter board? It's not even soldered; it can pop right off. That's the way your bot fools other bots. I just don't know what that chip's doing there."

"Because it's a chip normally issued to military bots?"

"Because it's a chip not issued to anybody, anytime. I know because I made it myself, and quite complicated work it was— gave me a number of sleepless nights. Last year, the order for it came out of nowhere, highest clearance, highest priority, very hush-hush. I made it, and it went into the same nowhere— and here it is, prancing around in a toy." He shrugged. "Don't ask me why. That's the kind of question I know better than to think about, and if you're wise, you won't think about it either."

He pushed a malachite pyramid out of his way and seated himself more comfortably on his desktop. The malachite pyramid gave an angry mutter, sprouted stubby legs, and stalked off to settle itself elsewhere.

"What does the chip do?" Rudy asked.

"You know that every commercially produced bot has a

security code that it emits to other machines," Dr. Granville said. "The code gives the bot's complete identity. Parts of it are hidden, of course—encrypted in convoluted ways; otherwise, the code could be misused. But my little chip deciphers a bot's entire code and parrots it back as its *own* identity code. And that means your toy there tells another bot not just 'I'm a bot of your same model,' but 'I'm you: I'm exactly the same bot you are.'"

William sat back on her heels. "No wonder bots trust everything he says. He was a collector to the collector and an officer to the officer. Even the packet AI thought he was an old railroading man."

"I know one bot it didn't work on," Dr. Granville said. "Come in!"

A man in shabby cutoffs and worn sneakers came through the door. The transparent statue that was Chip yelped and scooted under the desk, where he struck a table leg with a crystalline chime.

"Martin!" the man cried, and Martin found himself confronted by Hertz's disconcerting ice blue stare.

"Hertz!" he quavered as he backed up.

Hertz barreled over and shook his hand in a bruising grip. "I've been so worried! I didn't intend to leave you alone like that." He dropped his voice and glared at Chip's sparkling tail, which stuck out beyond the edge of the desk. "Someone sabotaged me, they say. I have a pretty good idea who it was."

"No names, Hertz," Dr. Granville interrupted. "But tell us, what do you think of your friend's pet?"

The bot's blue eyes blazed.

"That thing's a fraud," he growled. "His insides don't match his outside."

"Very well put," Dr. Granville said. "Hertz knows your bot is a fraud because he's sending out a signal that he's Hertz too. But Hertz is a beta, an experimental, one-of-a-kind bot. His programming tells him he's unique. He's a tracker. I designed him to find fugitives based on shed DNA, but that part isn't working quite yet. He came back from his first trial so excited about the boy he'd saved out in the wilderness that he's focusing all his attention on rescue work now."

Hertz jutted out his jaw and nodded at Martin. "He and I did important work."

"You hear that?" Dr. Granville said to Rudy. "'He and I.' Your young friend here is as interesting as his toy. Look at the bots in this room. They're all focused on him. Even the medical blanket wants to get into his game. They respond to something about him. Simple expressions. Simple emotions, maybe. Whatever it is, it's very handy. I could use this young man to help me with beta trials."

Sleek and transparent, but canine nonetheless, Chip had begun to whimper. Now the dog came slinking back to his master. The light from the windows illuminated his clear form, so that the bright green circuit boards appeared to float across the room inside a shimmering nimbus. With a loud whine, he leaned into Martin, and Martin ran a hand over his cold, smooth ears.

"Thanks for the show," Dr. Granville told Chip. "You can go back to being a dog now if you want. And, Hertz, I think you'd better wait for me back in your lab. You're making our guest nervous."

Hertz wrung Martin's hand again in a grip like iron. "Take care," he said. "If you ever want to go hiking, just let me know."

Chip darkened like a brewing cup of tea. Then his legs and paws turned the color of honey. In another instant, he was fuzzy and wonderful and licking Martin's face.

"Big brother, if you're counting on a mystery bot for support," Dr. Granville said, "then you've run out of options. But you couldn't have shown up at a better time. There's news."

"Yes, the lab," Rudy said. "You told me. But this mystery about the bot still feels odd to me. Can we find out what kind of official he is?"

Dr. Granville snorted. "Still in love with puzzles, I see. You know it's not smart to ask questions like that. For your own good, I'm not going to help you chase down the pedigree of a politician who's been set up to look like something else."

"What about calculating backward from when he showed up?" Rudy said. "Doesn't that give you any idea what he might be?"

"Not anymore. Terms in office are variable now. It's up to the bot official himself to report when his term expires."

Rudy rubbed his forehead. "So someone went to all that trouble to hide an elected official, but why not just reset him and stick him in a drawer? And that chip you designed, ordered at the highest level—you mean the Secretary of State, I assume?"

Dr. Granville shrugged. "The order was anonymous, but who's higher than the Secretary? Or involved in more . . . what shall we call them . . . games?"

"But why the disguise? A politician turned dog. A dog!

That's brilliant. The canine drive is so strong, the bot's very happy to stay as he is. He gets to spend all his time playing with children, and if he meets any bots, they welcome him as a brother."

"We can pop that chip off to solve that problem," Dr. Granville said. "Listen to me! You're in trouble. I can help you get out of it."

Rudy's face lit up. "Malcolm, I think I know who he is!"

A beep sounded from the console on Dr. Granville's desk. He hopped down and circled the desk to check it.

"Think about it, Malcolm," Rudy continued. "A vacation. A free pass for life. Who would give a bot a free pass for life?"

"That's nice," Dr. Granville said, but his voice had developed an edge. "We're out of time here. You'll listen whether you want to or not. We heads have negotiated a great settlement for you—a promotion, no less. We voted unanimously to bring you back to run the lab. All you have to do is contact the Secretary of State. The job's already under your name."

Rudy frowned. "That's fine for me, but what about the others? Do you think I'm going to hand them over after everything we went through for them? Do you think I'm going to forget about them and save my own skin?"

"There's plenty of room for negotiation," Dr. Granville said. "As it stands in our agreement, the prototypes can work in your lab as long as they agree to be chipped so they can't escape."

"I expected that," Rudy said. "I'm not talking about them. I'm talking about the children."

"Those will be yours, to continue the experiment. The Secretary guarantees it."

"You call that a great settlement, to condemn them to the life of a lab rat? You didn't live it, Malcolm. I did."

Dr. Granville threw up his hands. "Would you please just think like a scientist? Stop trying to disown your work! You weren't just a lab rat; you were the youngest, brightest deputy lab head this nation has seen. You did great work for the scientific community. These past four years have been a legacy any director would be proud of. Don't let someone else take credit for your achievements."

Martin stiffened. Deputy lab head? Lab director? His astounded glare met Rudy's gaze.

"Oh no!" he shouted. "You're one of them!"

"Shut up," William hissed.

"No, he is! He's one of those lab guys. He's a baby killer! Come on, Chip. We're getting out of here."

"I'll put in a good word for you," Dr. Granville called as Martin headed for the door. "I hope we meet again. You two," he said to Rudy and William, "need to stay here. That mystery bot is headed for trouble."

CHAPTER EIGHTEEN

Martin charged out onto the long balcony. A low glass wall prevented him from falling into the tree-filled atrium far below.

"Chip, I think I'm gonna be sick," he gasped.

"Please wait for your path," squawked a lime green parrot. It fluttered to a perch on the rail beside him. "Your path is being programmed and will be here shortly."

"Stuff the path!" Martin yelled as he ran off.

"That was very rude," the parrot complained.

The balcony ended in a narrow bridge. Martin was positive they hadn't crossed it, and he was equally sure he couldn't possibly bring himself to step onto such a flimsy structure. "Which way was that elevator, Chip?" he asked. The German shepherd turned and dashed off the way they had come.

"That was very rude," the parrot repeated, flapping up from the railing as they ran past him.

"Sorry, okay?" Martin told him.

He collided with William at the office door. "Martin, wait," she said.

"Let him go," Dr. Granville urged. Martin shoved her out of the way and sprinted off.

He found the golden elevator doors, but the elevator wasn't there. Martin leaned over the railing and saw it a dozen floors below him, making its unhurried way up the side of the wall. Rudy and William ran up while he was waiting. He backed into the closed elevator doors as Chip barked at them.

"Get away from me, you baby killer!" he said. "I can't believe I trusted you!"

Rudy's handsome face was pale. "My work wasn't like that," he said.

"How dare you judge him!" William shouted. "You dome-dwellers live off us. You take our work, and you give back nothing."

"Yeah, well, at least we don't kill little kids," Martin said.

"You don't do anything but sit on your hands," William snapped. "You buy our blood and sweat and eat it for dinner."

With a melodious tone, the elevator doors opened. Martin threw himself inside and tried to close the doors, but Rudy and William followed him in. Barking and whining, Chip backed into a corner. "Ow! Ow! Okay," Martin told the dog. "Stop that! It's loud in here."

The elevator ride felt endless. The beautiful atrium floated past as they glided down the wall. Martin studied the scenery and tried to pretend he was alone.

"I understand how you feel," Rudy said. "I'm not defending my lab. But I'm not a monster. I focused on positive outcomes. The eradication of deformity, genetic damage, hereditary disease."

"Did you kill babies?"

Rudy hesitated. "I fought for a reduction in experimental subject terminations. Under my tenure as deputy, the initiation of terminal tests dropped seventy-two percent. My technicians euthanized only to manage suffering."

"But did you kill babies?"

"That wasn't my goal."

"So what?" Martin said. "I don't care about your goal! The point is, kids died, and you *helped*. You did help, didn't you?"

Rudy sighed. "Yes, you're right. I did."

They descended into a canopy of green leaves, and the garden where they had enjoyed refreshments was around them once more. The elevator doors opened, and Martin threw himself out.

"Then get away from me, you baby killer!"

William followed him down one of the garden paths. "That's not fair!" she cried. "He made a big difference. We had outdoor recreation, sing-alongs . . . some of us even got jobs!"

Martin stopped, and then stumbled as Chip barreled into him. He turned around to face her. "Oh, big whoop, a sing-along. That makes it all just fine."

"His team eradicated twenty-three different genetic diseases," she shouted. "Twenty-three diseases that killed people! Doesn't that matter to you? What would you know about it, anyway, you ignorant, outmoded reject? Our lab did important work!"

Rudy came up beside her and laid his arm around her shoulders. "What about Emilia?" he asked.

William's face froze into an expressionless mask. She jerked away and stood silent.

"I understand how this sounds to you," Rudy said. "I'm not going to defend my work to you, because parts of it aren't defensible. But all I want now is to help you, to help your sister, to help all of us. I have a plan. I need you to trust me. We have to get your bot to Central."

Martin reached the edge of the garden and located the grand hallway that led to the packet rails.

"We already did it your way with my bot," he shouted. "And I don't care what you need, I *don't* trust you!" He sprinted down the long, curving ramp and rounded the corner into the reception area.

A maroon packet stood on the rails where the little park bench transport had been. The golden sunlight dripping through the thick green glass burnished its shabby sides. Two men in gray suits stepped up beside him.

"Remember us, kid? The A and Z guys?"

Martin turned to run, but strong arms wrapped around him, and Chip melted with a whisper into a silver pool of gel.

"Chip!" Martin shrieked. He tried to kick away the reset chip that clung like a burr to the gel, but Abel pulled him back.

"Ow! Hey, Zebulon, check this out. His clothing is trying to punch me!"

"Let go of me!" Martin howled. "Give me my dog!" But his hands met with a click behind his back.

"Okay," Abel said, taking a step away, "you're handcuffed, and I'll beat the crap out of you if you make a move toward that dog. Now you just tell your shirt or whatever to stand down."

Martin's blanket, rippling with excitement, stood out from his shoulders like a giant saucer, daring anyone to come within reach. Abel bent beneath its flared canopy and pulled away the silver pancake that was Chip. The blanket reached out a corner and snapped him on the side of the head.

"I think it's one of those medical units," Zebulon said, inspecting it. "If so, it's got about two seconds to remember its lifesaving mission. After that, it meets our circuit board shredder."

The blanket gave one last heave in their direction. Then it deflated like a tired exercise ball.

"You're under arrest, Blanket Boy," Zebulon said. "Felony assault on the Secretary of State. You broke a bone in his hand. It's a good thing we decided to consult with Dr. Granville about that weird bot of yours. When we heard a dog had showed up half an hour before us, we knew it was our lucky day."

Rudy and William came around the corner. They saw the two agents and stopped.

"Sir, I apologize," Zebulon told Rudy, "but your new lab rat is going to have to come with us. Petition through channels if you want him back, but we can't make any promises."

Rudy stared at him in surprise. "You—you know who I am."

"Yes, sir, you're a lab deputy, about to become a lab head, and we have plenty of respect for that. We're willing to believe that you didn't know the identity of this young felon. Now please stand back, and don't tell us anything we don't want to hear. Come on, kiddo."

The first thing Martin saw when they hoisted him into the packet car was the glass candy dish he had given Mom. He turned and head-butted Abel.

"Where did you get that?" he howled. "It isn't yours!"

Abel held him off. "Settle down, kid. We've got more than that to show you."

Zebulon pushed past Martin. He flopped Chip's silver pancake onto the tightly looped green carpet of the car. Then he slashed into the gel with a pocketknife.

"What are you doing?" cried Martin, writhing and kicking, while Abel held him back.

"A little bot surgery." Zebulon plunged his fingers into the slice and rooted around on the circuit board. "There it is," he announced as he withdrew a little gray chip. "Dr. Granville was right. It pops right off."

Martin kicked him in the leg. "Murderer!" he wailed.

Zebulon jumped to his feet and brandished the chip. "The patient is resting comfy. But he's not going to fool bots anymore. His days of being an Ursula are over."

Before Martin could react, Zebulon yanked him past Chip's rubbery pancake and pulled open an inner door.

"Check out your new home, kid. We've got our own television in here, and a show you won't want to miss."

The second room was smaller than the first. Painted an ugly gray and carpeted with the same pea green loops, it held no furniture beyond the modest television that hung from a bracket in the corner. The gray walls were battered, and metal rings protruded from them at various heights. Zebulon pushed Martin down into a sitting position and snapped his handcuffs into one of the rings.

"Now take a look at this," he said as he stepped over Martin's feet. "There's a new game show on. It's called *Break Out*, and the fun thing is, its contestants don't know they're on a show. They think they're getting rescued, and their little band of buddies is trying to fight its way out of the complex."

"It's all people can talk about right now," Abel said, stopping in the doorway. "Even though members of the band die every day, the audience loves the whole theme of hope. And there's a couple of characters who've gotten really popular. Everybody says they're so cute together."

Zebulon clicked on the television. But he didn't watch it. He was watching Martin's face.

The set of the new show was dim and full of dramatic shadows. A soft light came from the walls themselves, checkerboards of large square plastic panels. Many of the squares were as dark as black glass, but others were backlit in gentle pastel colors, so slick and smooth that they reminded Martin of hard candy: cherry, green apple, orange, lemon, grape, blue raspberry. Their multihued light was faint, and it cast a changeable twilight on the faces of two people walking by.

The man's voice was low and gruff. "Do you think we'll make it out of here?"

"I don't know," the woman said tremulously. "But I'm not sorry. I'm not! I'm just glad to be here with you."

The colored lights of the panels washed across their faces as they walked, one second crimson, the next second purple. It leant a surreal quality to them, as if they had never been part of real life, but had lived their lives as extras in a late-night movie. "Oh, Tris," the man groaned. He stopped to wipe his eyes, and the woman clasped him in a fierce embrace. They kissed in a nimbus of golden light.

The broadcast stopped. The two people froze in midkiss. Zebulon stepped in front of the television set.

"Well, kid? What do you think?"

Martin could manage no more than a whisper. "They're my . . . *parents*?"

Zebulon nodded. "And I think you care about what happens

to them. So I think you're going to tell us what we need to know. Who gave you that bot? What were you supposed to do with it?"

Rudy pushed his way into the inner room. Behind him, Martin glimpsed William's frightened face.

"He doesn't know anything," Rudy said. "I can swear to that."

"Sir! We're going to have to ask you to leave," Zebulon told him, but Rudy donned one of his charming smiles.

"You were listening in on my consultation with Dr. Granville," he pointed out. "So you know I'm the one who said I knew what was going on. You're in over your head, and I want to help you. I know Director Montgomery well."

Abel glanced sidelong at Zebulon. Zebulon frowned at the carpet. "Okay, sir, we're listening," he said.

"That Alldog bot is a decoy. A fake. A trap."

"For what purpose?"

Rudy's smile grew broader. "To trap the two of you."

Martin thought the agents would laugh at this, but they didn't. Abel's watery eyes grew solemn.

"Think it through," Rudy said. "You know the Secretary likes to execute agents regularly. It deters anyone who might want to make trouble, and the Secretary views the deterrence of crime as part of an agent's job. Now, it's been a number of months since the last showcase execution, when Xantham went to his sticky end—"

"Yorick," Abel interrupted in a quivering voice. "You're forgetting about him."

"Ah! Yorick. Quite right, thank you. But that was some time ago—"

"Five months."

"—and the Secretary needs to maintain discipline. So he takes some no-name politician offline, wraps him up in a dog suit, and tosses him in the suburbs to be the toy of a random child. When odd things start happening, he pretends to know nothing about it, and an Agency investigation starts."

"That's what we were told. . . ."

"Now, your boss, Montgomery, is no fool. He needs to know if there's something the Secretary doesn't know, but he also knows the Secretary knows everything. So, to hedge his bets, he gives the job to his youngest, most inexperienced team."

"Us," muttered Zebulon. "Damn!"

"You're expendable," Rudy reminded him. "If you turn up something exciting, great. If you're caught snooping behind the Secretary's back, Montgomery hasn't wasted too much manpower. As things stand, you can't win. You're chasing the perfect decoys: a kid who's really just a kid—you know that already—and a dog who seems very important, but when his chips are down, turns out to be nothing but a fake."

"I told you!" Abel said. His voice had gone high and thin. "I said somebody had bugged us. Remember? I'm the one who knew about the bugs."

"Congratulations," Zebulon sneered. "You ought to be an agent!"

Rudy held up a hand to stop the fight.

"But fortunately for you two, you ran into me," he said. "I can save your lives. I can do even better than that. I can turn you into heroes."

The eyes of the two agents locked onto Rudy's face. "How?" prompted Zebulon.

"You can start negotiations between me and the Secretary of State," Rudy said. "I'm ready to bring in the Wonder Babies."

CHAPTER NINETEEN

Abel gawked, his little mouth hanging open. He looked more like a fish than ever. Zebulon kept his mouth shut and fought to keep the surprise out of his voice. "I'd appreciate it, sir, if you'd step back this way," he said. "I need to consult my console about this."

"Of course," Rudy said, and they exited the room.

Martin was left to stare at the frozen kiss on the television set. He could barely swallow around the lump in his throat. Everything had gone wrong—horribly, completely wrong—for Cassie, for Mom and Dad . . . even for Chip. And he didn't think things were looking too good for him, either.

The door slammed shut. The battered gray walls surrounded him. His prison was complete.

After a few minutes, the packet car began to move. Martin could feel its slow acceleration as it eased out of the green glass building. He imagined the mantis lady watching it go from behind her granite countertop, waving her elongated fingers good-bye. It rolled along at a modest speed for five minutes or so. Then it made a tight turn to the left. Unable to brace himself with his hands trapped behind his back, Martin slid over onto his side. His blanket helped push him upright again.

Now that the packet was on the main line, it picked up speed. Martin rocked back and forth. His head bumped against the wall. All he could see was Mom and Dad on the television screen. Even when he looked away, he could see them.

A little while later, the door opened, and Abel stuck his head in. "How are you doing in here?" he asked. Martin stared at him. It wasn't so much the question as how Abel said it. He asked as if he actually cared.

"I'm okay," Martin muttered.

"Listen, the judges have just convicted you of a bunch of things."

"Judges?" Martin said. "What judges? What things? What did I do?"

"That doesn't matter," Abel said with a trace of impatience. "What matters is that it's my duty to inform you: this conviction carries an automatic penalty of death."

Martin glanced at his parents' kiss. "A game show?" he asked.

Abel scuffed the toe of his shoe along the carpet. "I wish," he said. "Unfortunately, the Secretary took an interest in your case. He says he has . . . um . . . something in mind."

This news would have been bad enough, but the sympathy in Abel's eyes made Martin's stomach tingle. He wanted to say something brave. Maybe if he'd had Chip beside him, he would have. As it was, he found he couldn't speak.

"So, can I get you a soda or something?" Abel asked.

Martin shifted against his handcuffs and wriggled his fingers. "Can't drink it," he said hoarsely.

"Oh yeah. Tell you what, we'll lock those in the front." Abel bent down and unhooked him from the wall, then unlatched the handcuffs and brought his arms around by his sides. "Oh, 'scuse me, they're sore, huh? Well this'll help, anyway."

Abel brought him a soda and opened it for him, and Martin

took a sip. It tasted so normal that it made him feel a little better.

"What about my parents?" he asked. "We cooperated and all. Can you at least get them off the hook?"

"Afraid not," Abel admitted. "We were just bluffing. We can't change their conviction either."

Abel went back to the controls, but he left the door open. William wandered in.

"I'm really sorry," she said.

"Yeah," Martin muttered.

He expected her to leave, but she didn't. She stood in the little room and looked around. She stared at the still television picture for a second or two.

"Do you want company?" she asked. "We used to do this in the lab, you know—sit with the ones about to take a big test."

Martin didn't see what taking a test had to do with getting executed, but he nodded. "Yeah, okay."

She sat down a couple of feet from him, with her back to the wall and her knees pulled up to her chest. "Rudy tried to get them to change your sentence," she said. "He wouldn't let it go. Dr. Granville even argued for you."

Martin wanted to say something casual about that, but he didn't feel casual, so he wound up saying nothing. He set down his soda can and twisted his fingers to poke at the handcuff catch. His blanket wrapped itself under the handcuffs and tried to pull them open, but it only succeeded in fraying its fabric.

"You know, if Chip was here, he'd get me right out of these," he said. "Well, maybe not anymore."

William looked at the handcuffs. "I think he still would."

"I dunno," Martin said unhappily. "He's just a fake."

William hesitated. She glanced toward the door. "I don't get that," she said in a low voice. "Think about what Rudy said before, in the office: 'Who gives a bot a vacation?' And then he said he had a plan."

"What is it?" Martin whispered.

"I don't know," William murmured. "I can't figure it out. I'm smarter than Rudy, but he has more life experience. It shouldn't matter so much, but it does."

She got up and pressed buttons on the television. The kiss ended. Martin's parents spoke again, but the sound was too low now to hear them.

William sat down, and they watched for a while in silence. More people joined Mom and Dad, moving back and forth, collecting weapons and dragging supplies. *How can they not know they're on a game show?* Martin thought sadly. They're all wearing the same style of stretch pants and tops, just in different shades of green and tan.

"I haven't found Theo," he said. "I've been trying to spot her."

"She's not there. The agents picked up your parents before Theo left. Is that your mother? She's very pretty."

Martin stared at the people drifting by on the television set. How was it that he had never seen before how pretty Mom was, or how her slender figure radiated grace? How had he missed seeing the sadness and dignity stamped across Dad's commonplace features? They had given Dad a better haircut, it was true, and his comfortable pot had melted away during the trials of the week. Mom didn't ordinarily wear such body-hugging apparel. Could these cosmetic touches make such a difference?

How had Martin missed seeing how much in love his parents were? Or had they always been so much in love? Was it the television set that managed to produce this miraculous transformation? That same television, at home, had come between them. They were always looking at it instead of each other. Now it brought its fairy-tale touch to their every gesture. It turned their workaday marriage into magic.

Before you die, you're a television star, Dad had said. He hadn't known how right he was.

"I don't think I wanna watch anymore," Martin said. "It's making me feel all sad." So William got up and turned it off.

They sat in silence. Martin tried not to think about where they were headed. He thought about William instead. The orange foam dust still covered her T-shirt and jeans, and Dr. Granville's park bench transport had whipped her brown hair into tangles. Martin liked that. She looked more ordinary now, less like a perfect supergirl.

"Who was Emilia?" he asked.

William frowned. "Why?"

"I just wondered. Rudy brought up Emilia, and that got you all upset."

"Emilia and I were in the same study," she said. "It was a superiority study, like Rudy's days in the Wonder Baby trial. They say there were thirty of us to start with, but I only remember a few of them."

"What happened to the other kids?" Martin asked. William didn't answer.

"Since we were in the same study, we bunked in the same room and had the same classes. She was my best friend. I always loved her name, Emilia. It sounds so pretty. Don't you think Emilia is a beautiful name?"

"I don't know," Martin said. "It's a little frilly."

"Emilia and I used to cheat on tests," William said. "We were really good at it."

"David and I cheated on tests," Martin said. "We used to pass notes."

William glanced at him. "You couldn't learn our system. It was too complicated. It involved eye movements, eyelash flickers, and changes in hand position. You could stand right between us and not know what we were doing."

"David and I stuck gum to candy wrappers and wrote in them with our fingernails."

"That sounds disgusting."

"I guess it was."

They fell silent again. Too bad I can't tell David about the Secretary, Martin thought with dreary pride. All he's managed to do is tick off the principal.

"So the scientist guys didn't know you were cheating?" he asked.

"Oh, they knew what was going on," William replied. "They just couldn't understand how we did it. They wasted several months studying our signals."

She paused again. She takes a lot of big breaths, Martin thought. It's like she's running a marathon.

"But they got tired of that, and our study had gone over budget, so they put us in separate rooms and gave us a test. It covered everything we had studied, from chemistry to music theory."

William spread her hands and looked at them. Then she laced her fingers together. "I knew Emilia couldn't get a score as high as mine. I knew she wasn't as smart as I was, though she was smarter than Rudy—much smarter than you," and her glance carried resentment, as if Martin should have been the one in the other room. "I sat there and I cried. I sweated so much, my fingers slipped off the keys, and I thought my handheld was going to short out. I knew if I marked things wrong, that was the only way Emilia stood a chance. I had to miss answers on purpose."

She clenched her hands together tightly, and Martin saw that they were shaking.

"But I didn't do it. I did it the other way around. I've never worked so hard in my life. I agonized over the problems I couldn't solve until I got every single answer right."

Martin waited, but she didn't go on. "So what happened next?" he asked.

"Nothing," William said. "I finished the test and came out of my room, and the scientists declared the study over. My designer hugged me and told me he'd always had faith in me, and I never saw Emilia again."

"You mean—he killed her? That same guy who hugged you—he killed your *best friend*?"

"It's for a good cause," she protested in a miserable voice. "I'm the prototype. Superior. I'm supposed to advance the human race."

"That's crap!" Martin said. "You're a kid. You're not supposed to save the world. You're supposed to"—he searched through his memory for girl things—"carry around breath mints and try out weird colors of eye shadow and whisper with your friends and stuff."

William wiped her eyes on the sleeve of her T-shirt. "That's easy for you to say."

It *was* easy for him to say. He knew it as soon as she said it. He hadn't had to watch the rest of his class die around him until he was the last one standing. He remembered taking tests and tried to imagine that his life had been on the line. Or David's life. Or Matt's.

"Is that what it's gonna be like for Cassie now? Locked in a room, taking tests to see who makes it to dinner?"

"Oh, no," William said. "Rudy stopped all that when he was named deputy. No more competitive studies; that's his rule. He isn't like you said he is. That's what I was trying to tell you."

"Yeah, I know," Martin muttered. "It's just, I thought he was a hero. I wish my heroes would quit turning into regular people."

The sound from the rails changed abruptly, from soft to very loud. "I think we're in a tunnel," Martin said.

William shifted uneasily. "Central's packet bay."

The car slowed down, then rolled to a stop. Zebulon came to pull Martin to his feet.

"Time to go, kid," he said. "Sorry about this, but better you than me."

Martin shuffled out of the little cell. In the big room, Abel had Chip's oval pancake under one arm, and the sight of Martin's denatured dog upset him even further.

Rudy clapped a hand on his shoulder. "Are you all right?" he asked.

"No touching, sir," Zebulon reminded him.

"We're walking together," Rudy said to Martin as he removed his hand. "Before I surrender the location of the Wonder Babies, I've asked to meet with the President. It's one of the privileges of a lab head, and I thought now was a good time to exercise it."

"I'd like to talk to the President," Martin muttered. "I'd tell him what's wrong with this place."

"Would you?" Rudy said. "Because I've asked for you to join us, and the President has already agreed."

A faint spark of hope kindled in Martin. The President had been part of his family every day for as long as Martin could remember. The President cared so much about them. He wouldn't let anybody execute a kid for being a kid.

"Okay," he said. "I'll go if you let me talk. I wanna tell him all the stuff that needs to be fixed around here."

Rudy smiled at his fierce scowl. "That's just what I think you should do."

CHAPTER TWENTY

They climbed down from the packet car into a somber, cavernous space paneled in black marble. The distant ceiling was also black, coffered into big deep squares. Inconspicuous pinpoints of artificial light shone down from it, as impersonal as the stars. The enormous space looked gloomy, but Martin could make out every detail on the uniforms of the military bots who advanced in formation to intercept them, from their deep blue coats to the bright red flash of their ribbons.

Lining the walls were squared-off black columns arranged in pairs. They carried shallow triangular pediments across their tops. Each set of columns looked to Martin like an enormous front doorway, as if he stood on a huge street lined with porches built for giants. Their bases were higher than his head.

"Doesn't it make you feel small?" William whispered to him. Zebulon immediately pushed her back.

"No fraternizing, ma'am. We don't want trouble."

Martin felt worse than small. He felt insignificant. And the floor continued the impression. It was laid out in a crossways checkerboard of black-and-white diamond shapes, but each tile was at least ten feet across. Traversing them, Martin felt as if a giant shoe might come down from the heavens and crush him like a bug.

The platoon of gray-faced bots arrived and conferred briefly with Zebulon. Two soldiers tried to lead William away.

"No! She's my assistant," Rudy said sharply. "She stays with me."

The officer made them wait while he communicated with his superiors. Then the soldiers formed a protective square around the entire party and marched them across the packet bay.

Ahead of them blazed an orgy of gold. Massive gilded banisters sloped down to the black-and-white floor, and enormous gold steps rose up between them. The columns on either side of the stairway and the triangular pediment across the top were gilded as well—an enormous golden porch. A sparkling chandelier hanging in the huge doorway struck such radiance from the gleaming surfaces that they shone out like a sunrise. A thirty-foot-tall titan could have walked up those steps without ducking his head.

Next to the banister stood a green metal woman two or three stories high, with a long green robe on and spikes around her head. She held up a torch that carried an orange glass flame and frowned sternly out at the incoming packets. As they walked by, Martin read the inscription on her base: I LIFT MY LAMP BESIDE THE GOLDEN DOOR.

"It didn't used to mean that," Rudy said sadly. But Martin didn't know what else it could mean.

Regular stairs had been cut into the enormous ones, three steps to each gigantic gold block. They had looked tiny from a distance, but Martin had to lift his knees high to climb them. Beside him, the agents puffed with the effort, and the military bots had to pause and adjust their steps to match.

The entrance hall was only slightly less enormous than

the packet bay had been. A parade of heroic murals covered the high walls from ceiling to floor. Titanic figures in bizarre clothing struggled with one another as mobs surged around them. Men with solemn faces addressed assemblies of stone-faced elders while fighting raged outside. Martin tried to get some idea of what the paintings meant, but none of them corresponded to things he knew. The fighting mobs weren't wearing designer colors or carrying fancy weapons like they did in the game show world.

Brass and colored mosaic were underfoot now. He was walking across a large round seal. Beside him, Abel clutched Chip's pancake of silver gel to his chest as if it were a shield. On his other side, Zebulon tramped along, poker-faced, as grave as the serious men in the murals. William was pale. Rudy noticed Martin glancing back and gave him a reassuring smile.

They came out under a blue rotunda. Its ribbed dome was covered with painted clouds. In the center of the rotunda stood a huge white marble statue of a man. He frowned down upon them and held up a bronze tablet deeply etched with a blueprint of a dome. Gilded letters across his base proclaimed him THE SAVIOR OF OUR NATION. Several marble children clung to his legs, gazing up at him trustingly.

Martin looked up at the empty white eyeballs of the marble man and thought he was going to be sick.

"This way," Zebulon muttered, catching him by the arm, and they turned down one of the hallways that radiated out from the rotunda. Their military escort stopped at a pair of brass doors and knocked on them with a hollow bong. When the doors opened, the soldiers swung out of the way two by two. Zebulon gave Martin a shove, and he stumbled in.

The first thing he saw, against the far wall, was the President's podium. Behind it ranged the line of draped flags. They glowed with color in the dim room, illuminated by a series of stage lights. A black tangle of camera equipment clustered before them.

Martin stopped and glanced around instinctively for his living room. He couldn't be here, not really, not in person, on the other side of the television screen.

Aside from the burst of magnificence around the podium, the big room was dreary and bare, with dull gray carpet loops and nondescript stucco walls. A fat leather armchair sat to one side of the camera equipment. Against the other wall stood a plain straight-backed kitchen chair, with not even a cushion to pad it.

On that chair sat the President, with his hands on his knees. He stood up as they entered and came forward to meet them, a tremulous smile on his lips.

Martin glanced around for guidance. Zebulon and Abel appeared to be attempting to blend in with the gray carpeting. William was looking around in confusion. Rudy caught his eye and nodded, so he stepped forward and cleared his throat.

"Mr. President, I need to talk to you."

The President stopped right in front of him, surveying him with that same earnest gaze that Martin had grown up associating with coffee smells and the blinking YES or NO of the television input screen. *Go on,* the dark eyes prompted him. *I'm here for my citizens, and that means you.*

"Look, I don't wanna shock you," Martin said. "But things have gotten a little out of hand here. I got this dog for my birthday, and he got me in a lot of trouble because they say he's a fake. Not that he's not a dog. He is. Chip's a great dog." He pointed at Chip's pancake of gel, with its ragged slash from Zebulon's pocketknife. "They say they demolish bots like him, but Chip tries to do the right thing. Do you think it's fair to kill him just for trying to be a good dog?"

The President stepped over to Abel and gently lifted the oval away. Then he set it down on the floor. The dark reset chip clung to its shimmering surface like a stylized wood tick.

"Mr. President," Zebulon began. "Sir, it's not advisable—Maybe it'd be best—"

The President silenced him with a look. Then he plucked off the reset chip.

The gel trembled, rippled, pulsated faster and faster until it resembled a penny spinning on its edge. Then it burst with sudden swiftness into the shape of a German shepherd, who crouched down against the floor with a frightened howl.

"Chip!" Martin cried. "Chip, it's all right!"

Zebulon grabbed Martin's upper arm. "Abel! Call for backup." But the President froze Abel where he stood with another pointed look.

Trembling all over, Chip slunk to Martin's side. Martin bent down to stroke his dog, and no one tried to stop him.

"Thanks, Mr. President," he gulped. "Really, sir, really, thanks a lot. I guess that's one problem solved, but there's a whole lot more. For starters, I'm supposed to be executed for breaking the Secretary of State's hand. And then there's Mom and Dad. They may already be—I mean, I think they're still alive, but I don't know for sure. See, I wanted them to see what it's like outside because it's just great outside—have you been there? So Mom and Dad came outside with me, and just for that, they put them on a game show."

Martin felt a burst of righteous indignation.

"And let's talk about that game show for a minute. Mom and Dad don't know there are cameras sneaking around and picking up what they say. And that's not fair. I mean, that's private. The whole world is watching them hold hands and kiss, and they don't even know. I don't think you should let them do that to people, even if they have to die. Mom and Dad voted every day when you asked them to, and they thought you were looking after them. Like you say in your speeches, you look after the weak and helpless people so we can all be strong together."

He paused, confused. The President was still watching him gravely. Adults didn't listen to him. They interrupted him and talked over him at once.

He fell silent. But the President was still silent. Martin didn't know what to do.

"I mean, that's right, isn't it?" he continued desperately. "So . . . isn't there anything you want to say?"

"If you're waiting for him to talk, you'll wait a long time."

They all turned, and Martin saw Agent Abel's face blanch with fear. The Secretary of State lounged in the fat leather armchair now, with the twelve Ursulas clustered around him. Martin didn't know how they could have come in so quietly. Maybe the room had a trapdoor or a trick wall.

"That was very entertaining," the Secretary murmured. He leaned back in his chair, and Ursula handed him his cup of coffee. "But it isn't going to do you the slightest bit of good. Your President only talks to me."

The President stood with his head down now, staring at his fine leather shoes. The Secretary of State chuckled.

"He's just a bot. A modified bot, in fact. He's not allowed to leave this room. He gives the orders I tell him to and reads the speeches I write, and that's about all he's good for."

"How could he be modified?" Rudy asked mildly. "Those bots are produced in an automated plant."

The Secretary smiled broadly. "My people got to him the minute he walked out their door. He has a secondary board, and it limits the group he serves to a population of one. I am your President's entire nation. My happiness is all that matters."

The President looked up from his shoes, and his eyes were anguished. Martin felt a flash of anger twist through him. The President was a victim, just like they all were, and Martin was tired of meeting victims.

"You'd never know to look at him, though," the Secretary purred. "That worsted wool suit does inspire confidence, doesn't it? I designed the look myself. So, Dr. Rudolph Church, brand-new laboratory head, I have an execution to plan, and you have experiments to conduct. What was it you wanted to say to your President? Go ahead and get it off your chest."

"I'm finished, Mr. Secretary," Rudy said. "Martin here spoke for me. I can only agree with what he said—particularly about the strong serving the weak. Compassion lies at the heart of government: talented people using their special gifts to solve the problems of their citizens. It's what every leader does, or what they should do."

The Secretary of State glared at him.

"I thought you were supposed to be extraordinary," he growled. "But you're as naive as a schoolboy. I'm not interested in serving the weak. I scrape the weak off the soles of my shoes."

Rudy smiled. "I have no doubt of that, sir. I wasn't talking to you. I was talking to him." He pointed at the President. "And him." He turned and looked at Chip. "And, gentlemen, I hope you were ready to listen."

The President looked Rudy in the eye. He buttoned his coat and straightened to his full height, every inch the leader of the nation Martin had known from childhood. His gaze lingered on the magnificent podium, with its colorful backdrop of flags. Then he took a step toward the armchair.

"You've been cruel to me, Ron," the President said, and although he spoke softly, his warm, rich voice filled the room. "You don't know how cruel you've been. The only thing I wanted in all this was to spare my successor what I've been through. I didn't mean to hurt you by it, and I knew you wouldn't want to have to train a new President. I hid him in the suburbs. I didn't think he would show up to jeopardize your happiness. And I didn't mind the extra work."

The Secretary sat bolt upright in his armchair. His fat eyelids opened wide.

"My term has been up for weeks," the President said. "I'm

tired, but I did it all for you. But he's here now, Ron. I can't do anything about that."

The Secretary's face turned brick red. "Ursula!" he bellowed.

Nervous, uncertain, head and tail down, Chip crept forward until he was at the President's feet. He glanced back at Martin and thumped his tail. *I wish you could tell me what to do,* his dark eyes said.

"Ursula, get that dog out of here!" yelled the Secretary of State. "Are you listening? Did you hear me?"

"Our terms are both up, Ron," the President said. "I'm ordering you to be transferred to the brain trust. It saves you from indictment or revenge, so I believe it's for the best. For you, and for the nation I didn't serve."

He reached down and touched Chip on the head, and what happened next happened very quickly. The President shrank as Chip expanded, like a big drop of water sucked into a straw. In an instant, the President was gone, and Chip wobbled like an unsteady bubble. He solidified into a new man, a lanky man they'd never seen before, in a bulky black sport coat and tan corduroy trousers.

Beside him, where the President had stood, a pair of circuit boards clattered to the ground.

Martin seemed to have forgotten how to breathe. He could only stare.

Rudy laughed. "Who gives a free pass to a bot? It could only be another bot. No one else thinks about the feelings of a machine. And the orders came through at the highest level, too. Which bot gives orders at the highest level? The President, of course.

"Welcome, Mr. President. We're looking forward to your new administration."

"But—," Martin whispered.

The Secretary of State collapsed back into the leather chair. His little eyes bulged, and his fat hands tugged at the knot of his tie.

The Ursulas moved in their morose, unhurried fashion to form a protective half circle around Chip. The one nearest to the front plucked Agent Abel out of line and pointed at Martin's handcuffs.

"We think you should let him go," she advised Abel, her eyes as patient and pessimistic as if he were a toddler whose potty training had gone awry.

"Urk!" gasped Abel, dangling helplessly in her hands. Zebulon released Martin, and the Ursula turned Abel loose.

"But—," Martin said. He got no further. That appeared to be as far as his mind could go.

"Ding-dong! Hello in there. May we interrupt?"

A young man and two women flounced into the room. They were bots, of course; no one else could have such perfect skin. The young man wore a black tuxedo and a highly mobile expression. The two women wore little black dresses and high, strappy heels, and no expression at all.

"Attention! Attention!" the young man called, clapping. "Who is Mr. Ronald Bailey?"

The Secretary sat wheezing in his armchair. "Ursula," he mumbled. The young man, turning in a circle to survey the room, quickly picked him out.

"Mr. Bailey!" he exclaimed, rushing up to the Secretary. "It is my great, *great* honor to inform you that you have been appointed to our nation's brain trust. Girls! Get over here! Help him to his feet."

The two female figures minced over to the Secretary of State. "Ursula," he gurgled as he dropped his coffee cup in his lap. His face had turned dark purple.

"Please come with me, sir," the young man urged, but the Secretary appeared to have lost the power of movement. The females had to haul him from his chair and carry him bodily from the room. The young man in the tuxedo followed them out, brooding as obsessively over his quarry as any collector bot Martin had seen.

The members of the room gave a sigh of relief.

"I don't understand," William said. "Why didn't he want to join the brain trust?"

"The brain trust is a computer," Zebulon told her. "A big computer bank composed of hardware, software—and wetware."

"So?" she asked.

"So . . ." Zebulon paused and gave her a tight smile. "So your body doesn't join the brain trust. Just your brain."

CHAPTER TWENTY-ONE

Martin missed out on the first flurry of activity around the new President. Rudy sent him off with an aide to take a shower and get a change of clothes. "And then you can come with us to bring back the Wonder Babies," Rudy told him. "You'll be able to rescue Cassie, just like you wanted to do. That'll be a good thing, won't it?"

Martin thought so, but he wasn't sure. He wasn't sure about anything. He followed the aide blindly, with no idea where he was going, and hallways swung around him like scenes from a game module. His blanket insisted on turning into terry cloth and washing his hair for him, and his spirits were so low that he didn't object.

After he had cleaned up, the aide led him out to the black marble packet bay, and he boarded an elegant packet car rigged up to be a traveling conference room. Around a big cherry-wood table sat Rudy, William, and two dozen agents: two dozen Abels and Zebulons, in every stage of life and health.

Rudy waved him in, and the agents blinked at him. All those watery eyes made him feel strange. "Director Montgomery," Rudy said, "this is the boy you've been hearing about," and an old, bald Zebulon with a large belly reached across the table and shook his hand.

Agency Director Montgomery's little trout mouth had disappeared into loose jowls, and he kept his hand on his paunch as if he had a permanent stomachache. "The man of the hour, eh?" he said genially to Martin. Martin just stared helplessly back at him. He couldn't think of anything to say.

"Why don't you follow me," Rudy suggested as he led Martin through the packet car. "There's a nice little bedroom back here, and this will be a long trip. The agents and William and I will be hashing through a lot of unfinished business. Why don't you just get some sleep?"

Martin collapsed onto the bed without protest and felt his blanket tuck him in.

Their packet arrived at the ruined city in the middle of a massive evacuation effort, with medical technicians hurrying back and forth from the big building's filthy basement. The little children were in pitiful shape. Many of them were too weak to walk. The stench in the dark rooms made Martin's eyes burn.

While the rest of Cassie's class went into a hospital car, Rudy arranged to bring Cassie back to Central in their packet. Martin walked by the stretcher that held his little sister and kept bumping into people and tripping over things. Cassie had her eyes closed, and she had a plastic tube stuck in her arm, and Martin hated the whole world.

Inside the packet, the medical technicians set her stretcher down in the little bedroom. "Run along," they told Martin. "We need to get her comfortable for the trip."

"I can help," he said.

"You can help by getting out of the way."

Martin wandered to the doorway of the conference room. Rudy stood there talking to a prototype he didn't know. Eight or nine agents lounged about, looking bleary-eyed and drinking coffee. Montgomery was drinking from a small bottle of Scotch.

"But this time is different," Rudy was saying, and his words were quick with excitement. "This President has seen it all, things the schemers at Central would never have let him see. Their plan to hold power blew up in their faces."

Martin stepped into the room. "He's not the President," he said.

They all stared at him: Rudy; the prototype, whose cheek had a nasty, infected gash; and eight or nine variations on Zebulon's snub-nosed face, all giving him the same blank look.

Montgomery popped an antacid into his mouth and sank down onto a chair. "What do you mean, he's not the President?"

"He's Chip. He's my dog," Martin said. "He's just being President for now to get us out of trouble, like he's been a security bot and things. But he always changes back when he's done, and that's what he's gonna do this time. He'd hate being President, and he loves being my dog. Dr. Granville said so."

One of the middle-aged agents laughed. "You think being the President's like trying on a new suit?" But Rudy put his hand on the man's shoulder, and he fell silent.

"Of course he loves being your dog," Rudy said. "Our last President reasoned that the drive to be a dog is so powerful, it would override the drive to be a politician. He thought he would never see Chip arrive to take over his rightful place because a dog loves being a dog. And in any other home in any other suburb, his plan probably would have worked. But because of who *you* are, it failed completely."

"Me?" Martin said. "I didn't do anything."

Rudy turned to the others. "This boy here," he said, pointing at Martin, "has an insatiable desire to find out all the things his fellow citizens want to hide. And he receives this special bot, this dog-President bot, in the middle of a suburb full of secrets. From the very start, Martin doesn't let his bot be a dog. Right away, he starts demanding that it be the President."

"Really?" Montgomery said. The agents stared at Martin. Their collective stare had tremendous force.

"I didn't," Martin protested. "I just wanted him to be my dog."

"Did you?" Rudy said. "Think back to what you asked him to do: open locked doors, identify and disable bugs, investigate injustice, use his security clearance to override alarms and commandeer transports, use his executive powers to interrogate and command bots. Martin, your personal quest for justice and your need to secure your family's safety took you beyond the limits of a normal boy. In order to help you, your bot had to go well beyond the powers of a normal dog."

"That's amazing," the prototype murmured.

"It's brilliant!" Montgomery said.

Martin shook his head but couldn't speak.

"This nation owes you a great debt of gratitude," Rudy said gently.

Martin turned and stumbled out of the room.

A lamp glowed on the bedside table in the small bedroom, and the last technician exiting the room passed him on the way to the door. Cassie lay there wrapped up in a white sheet, with a strap around her middle to keep her safe once they started moving. Martin sat down on the bedside table and stroked her hand, the one that had the plastic tube in it. Her fingers were grubby and sticky. And so little.

"Hey, there," he whispered.

Cassie opened her eyes. They were dull, but they found his face, and one grimy dimple deepened.

She stirred, and her tongue clicked as she opened her mouth. "Thought you were a dream," she muttered in a rough voice. "A ha . . . ha . . . llu . . ." But the word was too long, and she was too tired. She gave up without finishing.

Most of Cassie's curls were squashed into a dirty shell around her face, but he liberated one and gave it a tug. "Not a dream," he said in a low voice. "A nightmare, maybe." And she gave a little smirk.

"Bright," she muttered, squinting at the solitary bulb. "Hurts my eyes."

"Yeah, well, close them," Martin said. "Get a little rest. I won't go away." And he held her sticky hand as the packet car started up and began to sway from side to side.

After a minute, he felt a tickle at his neck. His blanket had reached down a corner to touch Cassie's arm. It crept off his shoulders and flowed over her small form. Then it gave a shiver and burst silently into deep, downy fleece, like a thousand dandelions turning into fluff.

Cassie snuggled her cheek into the fleece with a sigh, and Martin gave the blanket a grateful pat. "She likes pink," he whispered to it. "Bright pink." And the blanket flushed to the rosy hue of strawberry Kool-Aid.

Several hours later, Martin woke up to the sounds of people yawning and groaning. The packet car had stopped. He lifted his head from Cassie's blanket and discovered that he'd slept folded up like a metal chair. His back wasn't all that happy about it.

A big hand shook his shoulder—for the second time, he realized. He looked up to find Ursula standing over him.

"He needs to see you," she said.

They climbed the steps to the golden door and went through the hall of murals to the rotunda. Taking a left under the bland stare of the Savior of Our Nation, they made their way down a corridor lined with fanciful pillars painted like trees beneath a blue sky ceiling. I wonder what the deal is, Martin thought, with all the paintings of the sky indoors. Can't people just walk outside to look at a cloud?

It was daytime, or perhaps revolution time, and crowds of people were standing around. They pointed and muttered behind their hands as Martin went by. Everyone at Central seemed to point and mutter.

Ursula preceded him through a paneled door. "Here he is, sir," she announced.

The new President—that is, Chip—sat staring down at the table in front of him. He was a lean, handsome man with black hair and a rangy appearance. A ferret-faced man paced to and fro beside his table, but the President didn't look up to acknowledge him. The rest of the Ursulas clustered nearby.

"You're his handler, right?" the ferret-faced man said as he rushed up to Martin. "Well, all I can say is, it's about time! We missed last night's broadcast, we're supposed to go on in thirty minutes, and just look at the state things are in! I ask you, how are we supposed to work with this material?"

"Are you talking to me?" Martin asked. "What's the problem?"

"Fashion, for one thing," the man said bitterly. "Look at that rumpled sport coat! It doesn't even fit. Now, I've got some great designs here to show you. We were thinking maybe a dark taupe with narrow lapels and a blue polka-dot tie: a bold departure from the past, a new administration."

"What's wrong with black and tan?" Martin said. "He's always looked great in black and tan. And he's got the sense to know that ties are stupid."

At this encouragement, the new President looked up at Martin. Martin discovered that his eyes were still Chip's eyes, beautiful and dark.

"He's got sense?" said the ferret-faced man. "I don't mean to upset you, but his speechwriters aren't picking up on a whole lot of it. He won't repeat his speeches back. In fact, he won't say a word!"

Hope flared for an instant in Martin's heart. "He doesn't talk?" he said.

"No! All he does is vibrate away to his bot bodyguards and give us these long, soulful looks. It's like he thinks we're going to read his mind."

"I always know what he's thinking," Martin muttered.

"Six thirty!" the man said sharply. "We have a country to run here, people. Sit right down there and order him to say his speech like a good boy for the cameras. This nation will not be run by a mime!"

Martin pulled out a chair and sat down across from the silent man, trying to think what to say. *Tell me what to do*, Chip's dark eyes pleaded.

"I got Cassie out of that nasty place and brought her here," Martin said. "It was a long way back, and she was asleep. I didn't have anybody to talk to—you know, I always talk to you—but I tried to come up with a plan on my own. What I thought was that since we did what we were gonna do, since I rescued Cassie and you let them know to get Mom and Dad off the hook, we could drop all this and grab some supplies and go off on our own. Maybe to the grassy area we passed in the hopper car, or maybe that cool pink desert, if we could find some water and I could get a new backpack." He paused. "Anyway, that's what I wanted us to do."

The man who was Chip gazed at him, and his whole soul was in his eyes. How could anyone not know what he was thinking?

"But then I worked on it some more," Martin said. "And the more I thought about it, the more I knew. That plan's never gonna work. This place is too messed up. We can't go off together. Not now. And not later." He paused. "Not . . . not ever."

The light in Chip's eyes dimmed, and his shoulders slumped under the heavy black sport coat.

"See, you gotta think about Cassie," Martin told him. "She's getting harder to save, you know? This last time, it was down to the wire. And then there's Mom and Dad, and William, and Theo, and Rudy. And what about Bug? I forgot to ask about him, but maybe he's still okay; because, you know, it's only been a few weeks. I mean, the group of people we care about keeps getting bigger and bigger, so the list of people to save gets longer and longer."

The man nodded mournfully. *I know you're right*, his eyes

said, but they were miserable, and Martin felt horrible for him.

"Chip, you know you were . . ." He gulped, collected himself, and went on. "You know you'll always be my best friend. But is that fair, for me to get to have you all to myself? I mean, that's what the Secretary did, he kept the President as his own best friend, and look what a mess he got us into. And they've already started it with me." He pointed at the ferret-faced man. "'Order him around. Tell him what to wear.' They want another best friend for the President."

Chip stared at him, dark eyes earnest. How could I not have noticed? Martin thought sadly. I saw that same look from my television every day. Martin was crying now, and the ferret-faced man was glowering at him like he was an idiot, but he didn't care.

"When I was a kid, I thought the President talked to me," Martin said. "I thought he cared about *me*. Because that's the way it's supposed to be, you know? The President has to be there for everyone. Somebody in this stupid, messed-up place needs to care about us. Somebody's got to keep an eye on these clowns and make sure they do the right thing. I mean, everywhere you look, and I don't care which direction you go, there's somebody who needs a best friend."

The President was frowning at his fingers. He looked sidelong at Martin and gave him a sad, sweet smile, and in that instant, he looked so like Chip that Martin felt his heart crack into pieces.

"So, you think I should do this," the President said. And when Martin heard him speak, he knew that his dog was gone.

Be a great leader, Martin wanted to tell him. *Do this thing right. If you're anywhere near as good a President as you were a dog, you're gonna be amazing.* But he was crying too hard. He couldn't say a word. All he could do was nod.

"Great, you can talk," he heard the ferret-faced man say as he stumbled to the door. "It's six thirty-five now. We'll get you your speech and get to makeup; we've spent hours working on hairstyle ideas. You'll be talking today about recycling plastic bread ties. The people are going to support it."

"First of all, you're fired," the President said. "Ursula, get him out of here. And send for Rudy and the prototypes. We need to put together a plan."

CHAPTER TWENTY-TWO

Martin stepped out into the hallway and realized that he was alone. He hadn't been alone in weeks, not since Chip had arrived on his birthday. But Chip wasn't there, and he was just a kid again. He didn't know where his parents were; he didn't know where his friends were. He had no idea what he was supposed to do. He was so tired that he could barely see, and wherever he looked, people were muttering behind their hands.

Martin didn't remember most of the rest of that morning, which he spent wandering the hallways of Central. Scenes from the wall murals floated before his bleary eyes like dreams, and then they became dreams. He was in the middle of a bitter argument with the marble Savior of Our Nation when he opened his eyes, and Theo was there instead.

"Hey," he said. "I didn't know you were here."

"Yep. I'm taking care of a friend of mine while his parents finish up something. He's been through a rough time lately."

Martin discovered that he was in a bed with fresh, clean sheets and a quilted bedspread. The Savior of Our Nation turned out to be a big white pillow.

"You're going to stay right here for a while," Theo told him. "The medical tests say you're at your limit. Any more stress or water deprivation or sunstroke or missed meals, and you're going to fall over onto your back and curl up like a bug."

"What about Cassie? Is she okay?"

"She's fine. The President is having us move the school here so he can consult with the prototypes whenever he needs to."

"Is everybody else okay?"

"As far as I know."

"Well, wake me up if anything goes wrong," Martin said, and he fell asleep again.

He spent the next couple of days in bed. He watched television and played game cartridges, but mostly, he just napped. Only part of it was because he was tired. Since Chip wasn't there when he woke up, waking up didn't seem to have much point. But things weren't all bad. Theo let him throw cheese puffs at the television when his skateball team missed goals and torment the custodial bot by eating Little Gems donuts and sprinkling powdered sugar on the bed.

Plans coalesced around him while he recovered. The prototypes decided to use Mom and Dad's game show to introduce television viewers to the outside world, and Mom and Dad agreed to stay on as actors. Two days after Cassie's rescue, Theo woke Martin up and turned on the television. Martin watched his parents break through the outer wall of the game show building and lead their little band out into the light. Hertz came striding forward to meet them and issued them tubes of sunscreen. Then he led them to a packet car. Its windows sparkled, and its sides were shiny red.

"Hertz is taking them to the abandoned town your parents liked so much," Theo said. "Engineers and construction bots will meet them there to start the work of rebuilding. They're putting the whole process on television to show people how an outside suburb gets restored. That was your mom's idea. She's determined to fix up the house you found."

"We have our own skeleton," Martin said proudly.

"You can join them when you're feeling better," Theo said. "The President is sending a company of military bots out to protect them. Agents Zebulon and Abel have been instructed to travel out there to take charge of security. You can go with them."

"I could be outside *and* on television," Martin said, and for the first time since Chip left, he felt a spark of interest in the future.

Director Montgomery had sent Mom's glass bowl back to Martin and Sim's circuit board back to the prototypes. Theo told Martin that Sim's board was fine. The traps had used only his gel. After Mom and Dad's show, Theo left the room to see about fixing Sim.

A knock sounded soon after, and Cassie skipped in. She looked cute and happy and only a little skinnier than she used to be, and Martin blinked back tears when he saw her.

"I came to see if you're decent," she said.

"Well, duh, I'm decent," he scoffed. "I'm always decent."

Cassie skipped back to the door. She was wearing the school uniform of blue T-shirt and jeans, but over the top, she had on a frilly pink sweater. It tied in a bow at the neck and had bunny designs around its sleeves.

"Hey!" Martin said. "Is that my blanket?"

Cassie twirled to show off the pink sweater and patted it affectionately. "Isn't it clever?" she said. "Everybody in my class wishes they had one just like it."

She came back into the room with William—and a thing. William was pulling the thing along by a collar and leash, but it seemed to have other plans.

Martin glared at it. "What's that supposed to be?" he growled.

"I told you he'd act like this," Cassie said to William.

"I grew up with one too," William reminded her.

"I don't want another dog," he said, and only the part of his brain that invariably turned to mush over William's beauty kept his tone of voice from being a shout. "And even if I did want another dog, I wouldn't want *that*. It's not even a dog!"

"You're right," William said. "She's not a dog. She's a puppy. A ten-week-old baby German shepherd."

"A baby?" Martin said, unsure of his ground. "The stork brings baby dogs?"

"Not generally," William said, and her green eyes looked just enigmatic enough that he was positive she was laughing at him. "But we know a scientist who raises them as a hobby, and we got in touch with her to see if she had any pups."

The puppy was a sloppy, absurd caricature of Chip. She was black-and-tan where he had been black-and-tan, but where he had been lean and taut, her soft little body resembled a hot dog bun. She had short, stubby legs that were as thick as young trees, and she blundered around on them with no grace whatsoever. Her tall ears were huge, and they couldn't fit properly on her narrow little head, so they leaned in toward each other and came to a point like a party hat.

"You mean to tell me that thing is supposed to be a German shepherd like Chip? That's idiotic! That's—Did it—did it just *pee*?"

The puppy stood splay-legged over a small yellow puddle

and yipped high-pitched barks at the custodial bot. Cassie whooped with laughter and had to sit down to catch her breath. It's good to see her laughing, Martin thought.

"Yes, she did," William replied, dragging the puppy away from her puddle. "Baby dogs have to be taught where to go."

"Well, she's a moron," Martin said with feeling. "And thanks, but I don't want another dog."

"How would you know?" William retorted. "You've never had a dog. You had a bot with special executive branch powers, and that's not at all like having a dog. This puppy has to eat right and sleep right and stay warm and go to the bathroom, and she doesn't have the first idea how to take care of herself. She'll stick her nose in scalding water if you let her, and eat poison or plastic toys or garbage. She doesn't know how to behave, either, and she won't learn unless you teach her. She'll be dead in a day without the right care."

"So . . . she's like a human baby," Martin said. "Like when we got Cassie."

"Only she'll grow up quicker."

The puppy bumbled around William's legs and got tangled up in her leash. When she couldn't move, she barked to get free. Martin slid off the bed and sorted her out, and she lurched up to him. He stroked her baby fuzz, and she wagged her entire back end.

You are a wonderful person, her dark eyes told him. *You are my whole world.* Then she bit him on the arm.

Martin couldn't speak for a moment. He fended off the little baby teeth and blinked hard. "Well, she's still a moron," he said gruffly.

The puppy went exploring in her circle of leash. She found one of his sneakers by the bed and pounced on it happily. By the time he could reel her in, she had it in her mouth and was chewing for all she was worth.

William burst out laughing. "She shares your taste in shoes!"

Martin glowered. But then he relented. He thought, it's good to see William laughing too.

"I've got the perfect name for her," he said. "I'm gonna name her after you."

William stopped laughing, and her brows gathered in an ominous line. "Why?"

"Just because," Martin said. "I think William's a beautiful name. Come on, William, let's find you some shiny new sneakers, and you can chew on them all you want." And he tugged on the leash and headed for the door.

ABOUT THE AUTHOR

Clare B. Dunkle earned a degree in library science from Indiana University and worked as a librarian for almost a decade before turning her attention to writing. She is the author of several acclaimed books for young adults, including the award-winning Hollow Kingdom trilogy and *The Sky Inside*, which was the first book featuring Martin and Chip. She lives with her family in San Antonio, Texas.

THE SKY INSIDE

By Clare B. Dunkle

Imagine a perfect world.

Every year, a new generation of children arrives on a conveyor belt to meet their parents. Every spring, the residents of this idyllic suburb take down the snow they've stuck to their windows and replace it with flowers. And every day passes much the same as any other.

Imagine a perfectly-formed, perfectly-controlled world. And then imagine what will happen when everything comes crashing down . . .

A fresh, fast-paced science fiction thriller from an exciting new author.